Planet after planet falls to Soleyla's revolution, aided by the slaves who rally to her cause. Now the only hurdle remaining is the conquest of Argulus, the capitol planet of the Nine-Star League, ruled by Soleyla's mother.

In a deadly face-off between mother and daughter, Soleyla finally learns the shocking fate of Danel, her first pleasure slave — and discovers that Rachel Devarian holds Kantou's fate in her cold grasp as well. Can Soleyla find a way to save her beloved Kantou, or must she sacrifice the man she loves to save the galaxy from her mother's tyranny?

This book was previously published many years ago and has been reedited for publication.

WARNING: Contains explicit sexuality.

Devarian Revolution
Copyright © 2023 Sierra Dafoe
ISBN: 978-1-4874-3932-3
Cover art by Martine Jardin

Published by eXtasy Books Inc

Look for us online at:
www.eXtasybooks.com

DEVARIAN REVOLUTION
DEVARIAN CHRONICLES 3

BY

SIERRA DAFOE

PROLOGUE

Thunder still boomed, rolling away like the fading drumbeat of a massive army. Behind it, like tears, the rain came sheeting down, a heavy hissing fall that splashed into the watery mud and sizzled in the flames licking at the destroyed barracks. Soleyla barely heard it. Mindlessly, she lifted her sword again, driving it down into the corpse at her feet over and over in a frenzy of wrath.

"Captain, that's enough!"

Someone seized her arm. Quick as a snake, Soleyla spun, swinging her blade in a deadly arc at the intruder. Leaping back, Liatra raised her sword. The two weapons clanged together, ringing like a gong through the downpour. As if the sound had snapped the iron core of her rage, Soleyla sagged forward, dropping her sword into the mud.

"Why?" Her voice was no more than a whisper. She stared down at Valda's mangled body, feeling nothing but a vast, aching emptiness where her heart should be. The League commander's gaze was turned to one side, her dead features forever fixed in a triumphant sneer. "Oh, Liatra, why?"

The League base was in ruins, the hard-packed earth within its plasteel walls churned to muck, littered with bodies and shards of twisted metal from the shattered comm tower. Valda's surviving Guardians were huddled in a defeated cluster outside the command center, surrounded by the Antorean men.

But Valda had still won. Kantou was gone.

"We'll find him, Soleyla."

"Find him?" Soleyla lifted her head. Rolen was watching her, his blue eyes dark with compassion. Hideously, she began to laugh. It was a choking, bitter sound, cutting and cynical, spiraling dangerously close to hysteria. "*Find* him?"

Liatra slapped her, hard. Her hand cracked across Soleyla's high, broad cheekbone. "Captain, this isn't the time!"

For a moment, all Soleyla could see was red. But Liatra was right—it *wasn't* the time. Relief flickered in Liatra's eyes as she watched her captain slowly regain control.

"What are your orders?"

Breathing deeply, Soleyla straightened. "Send Marda to power up the advance ship. I want the Guardians in the command center under guard. If any of them will join us, so much the better. We need seasoned fighters. You'll know who we can trust."

Bewildered, Liatra asked, "Trust to do what?"

"To help us overthrow the Nine-Star League." Soleyla felt a cold satisfaction at the shock in her lieutenant's eyes. Then, before the jagged emotions inside her could tear themselves loose again, she turned away, walking carefully as if carrying something cracked but precious, something that might shatter entirely at one more blow.

It felt like being forced backward through a white-hot sieve. Flares of agony seared his back, as fresh and immediate as when the whip was first laid across it. His scars blazed with bitter, pulsing pain. Screaming, Kantou fell through a whirling, fiery torment, felt something like a wall of wind buffet him, and tumbled, stunned, onto the ground.

Hard, cold pavement pressed against his throbbing back. The two made a counterpoint of sensation he fixed on, clinging to them as he gasped, sucking in air, trying to control the sickly vertigo that wrenched at his guts. He heard startled voices, but they were distant, meaningless, muted by the throbbing in his head. Sunlight pierced his eyes, and he shut them.

Then rough, strong hands were hauling him up. His limbs were like water. He hung limply in their pinching grasp and fought not to vomit. Slitting his eyes, Kantou saw a Guardian towering over him, her face dark with fury. Two others were holding him, their hands clamped on his clammy, sweating skin. If they released him, he knew he'd fall.

"Who are you, slave? How did you get here?"

Kantou shook his head, unable to answer for fear of losing control of his gorge. Sparks of memory whirled through his brain—the roar of thunder, the stinking char of bodies, the echoes of Soleyla's final scream.

Kantou!

He swiveled his head, attempting to get a glimpse of the portal behind him. If it was still open . . .

A hard, gauntleted fist cracked across his cheekbone. Kantou reeled backward, kept upright only by the hands clenching his arms.

"Answer me, slave! What have you done to the portal?"

It was closed, then. He'd succeeded. The Guardians couldn't get through.

Relief roared through him, twisted together with a longing so profound it shattered what little control he retained. Lolling forward, he vomited on the hard white concrete, hearing gasps of disgust as the thick, vile liquid hit the pavement and splattered. The Guardian who'd struck him stepped back hurriedly, a revolted sneer on her face.

Soleyla had still been alive when Valda pushed him through the portal. His strong, beautiful Soleyla. If the portal had still been open, he would have done anything, would have fought his captors, bare-handed as he was, for a chance to plunge back through it to Antoros, to Soleyla . . .

If she was even alive.

Kantou sagged in the grip of the Guardians, almost wishing they'd let him fall. He squeezed his eyes shut, feeling a desperate prayer welling from the depths of his soul.

Please, let her be alive. Whatever happens to me, let her be alive.

A boot slammed into his abdomen, and this time he *did* fall, scraping his hands on the hard white concrete as he caught himself. The iron-faced Guardian kicked him again, and he tumbled to his side, writhing in the warm, sticky pool of his own vomit.

It didn't matter. There was nothing left for him now. Alive or dead, Soleyla was gone, far beyond his reach. There was nothing worse they could do to him.

"Take him to the senator." Kantou heard the words, but they had no meaning. The world around him was empty, hollow, a formless play of light stretched over a gray, howling emptiness. Even death held no terror for him. He would welcome its release.

But as they dragged him upward, Kantou saw in the distance a massive stone building, squatting at the feet of snow-capped mountains whose jagged outlines he knew, he *knew* . . .. Horror raced along his limbs, filling them with a feral, futile strength, and Kantou shrieked, fighting like a wildcat as the Guardians dragged him across the concrete toward the Priory of Argulus, the seat of the planetary regent—the cold, towering, stone-clad home of Rachel Devarian, First Senator of the Nine-Star League.

CHAPTER ONE

"No." Soleyla's tone was flat, final. Rolen stared at her incredulously, feeling a dismay so deep he couldn't begin to grasp it, bound together with a sudden, flaring rage.

"So that's it, then? You're not even going to *try* to find him?" Rolen pushed himself to his feet, glaring at her across the plasteel conference table. Around them, the ship hummed, its massive engines pulsing as it hurtled through the silence of space, powering up for the jump to interstellar. The light strips along the ceiling betrayed the circles under Soleyla's eyes, the lines of strain that marred her forehead.

Rolen didn't care. That was all Kantou had ever been to her, then. A slave. A possession. Something to use, and use, and then discard like a broken toy . . .

Just as the Guardians had used him. Rolen felt fury like a poison inside him at the memory, coupled with a wave of lust so thick it made him dizzy.

What had they done to him? And gods, had he *liked* it?

Around the table, the others shifted uncomfortably. Marda. Jerril, who had refused Rolen's order to stay behind and police the handful of Guardians who'd been left on Antoros. Liatra, who watched him, her hazel eyes dark with some unspoken protest.

There'd been Guardians all around him, pinning him to the ground. Their breasts had dragged, full and heavy, against his skin while their juices smeared his thighs, his chest, his face. He'd lapped hungrily, lost in the press of aroused flesh against his own, consuming them, being consumed . . . Their bodies had writhed against him, their slick vaginas and swollen clits thrust eagerly toward his seeking fingers. Every nerve in his body had screamed with unreleased need — and still they'd kept touching him, and teasing, and taunting, and demanding, until his entire body had blazed with overloaded sensation . . . Gods! He couldn't stop remembering the feel of their hands on his throbbing flesh, the sickly sense of terror and helplessness that had twisted just underneath that incandescent arousal — was *still* twisting like a snake in his guts.

And so was his desire.

Soleyla had done this to him, damn her. She had used him, just as she'd used Kantou, had flung him before the sex-starved Guardians like bait before a tiger.

Now she sat at the head of the conference table, her head held rigidly erect by neck muscles that stood out like taut cords, her eyes cold, expressionless, not even deigning to acknowledge his anger. Rolen wanted to slap her.

"You're going to just leave him. He saved every one of us and now you're going to abandon him. He could be hurt, for all you know. He could be —"

"Dead. Yes. I know."

Soleyla looked up at him. Something flickered deep in her eyes, an answering rage, perhaps. Rolen hoped so. He wanted to fight, wanted some way to discharge the seething morass of tangled emotions inside him. He sneered, his lip curling above his clenched teeth, and drawled, putting every ounce of disdain he could muster into his voice, "You never gave a *damn* about him, did you?"

"Enough!" Slamming her palms to the table, Soleyla sprang to her feet. She leaned on her arms, quivering with outrage. "I will not jeopardize this ship and everyone on it for the infinitesimal chance that we might find Kantou. What would you have me do, Rolen?" Her emerald eyes blazed with fury. "Crisscross the galaxy in a fruitless search until

Admiral Amista and every ship of the League descends on us and wipes us from the universe? Is *that* the task you asked your men to risk their lives for?"

Her words lashed him, cutting and effective. Feeling as if the floor had just dropped away, leaving him naked and ashamed before the entire galaxy, Rolen flushed. His anger balked within him, not dimmed, only shunted aside.

Slowly, Soleyla drew herself upright and turned to Marda, her voice once again harsh with control. "We will continue, as planned, at all speed for Harth. Our only hope of success lies in stealth and surprise. Alert me when we're leaving interstellar."

She strode from the conference room, leaving a tense silence behind her. Marda rose, gave Rolen one contemptuous glance, and headed back for the bridge. Jerril, red to the roots of his long blond hair, rose. His gaze flicked uncomfortably around the room, refusing to meet Rolen's.

"I, uh . . . I'd better check on the men." His voice ended on an uncertain lift, as if the statement were a question. Clenching his jaw, Rolen nodded, and Jerril, with an air of almost palpable relief, slid from the room. Rolen stared after him, his jaw clenched. She was leaving Kantou. After all her fine words, after all he had done for her. For *all* of them . . .

"Does she even have a heart?"

The words were murmured to himself, but Liatra answered behind him. "Don't judge her too harshly, Rolen."

He turned. The stocky, honey-haired lieutenant stood, her gaze resting on him worriedly. She laid a gentle hand on his arm, but he shook it off and turned away.

"Judge her? Why should I judge her? The woman will do anything, sacrifice any*one*, to get what she wants."

"And what does she want, Rolen?" Liatra's voice was still gentle, but there was a sudden, uncompromising edge beneath it. "Tell me, what is it you think she wants?"

Facing her again, Rolen was stopped by her mild expression. Whatever emotions she felt were well contained, but he sensed they were deep, deep as the roots of mountains, and as impossible to move. A memory stirred in him then, of those same quiet, steady eyes holding his gaze, seeming to pour along that nebulous contact all the strength and conviction contained within her sturdy frame.

Through the entire rape, she had been there, a constant presence beside him, doing her best to distract him when the sensations became overwhelming, trying to help him contain his inevitable orgasms. Single-handedly, she had fought to keep him alive.

Rolen felt tears come, stinging, to his eyes, and looked away. "You tell me, then," he muttered, his voice sounding surly and petulant even to himself. He owed her gratitude, he knew—and the knowledge only increased his discomfort.

Liatra was silent a moment. When she spoke, her voice was oddly distant, as if she were speaking to someone else entirely, someone not in the room. "Do you know why Soleyla was sent to Antoros?"

Rolen made no response, but she continued, her gaze fixed, as his had been, on the door Soleyla had so recently left through. "She refused an order. Her . . . commander"—and Liatra's pause made him wonder what word she'd been about to say instead—"took her pleasure slave as punishment."

Rolen snorted derisively, and Liatra turned to him, her eyes luminous with distress. "Believe me, I know how that must sound to you, Rolen."

There was something in the way she said his name, something tremulous and reaching, that cut through his disdain.

"But Danel was . . . special to Soleyla. She . . . Oh, how do I explain? She loved him. Not as she loves Kantou—and make no mistake, Rolen, she *does* love Kantou. But Danel was her first. Her friend. Perhaps the only friend she's ever truly had."

"Not you?"

He couldn't have said why he asked that. There was a flicker of pain in Liatra's eyes as she shook her head. "She doesn't talk to me. She doesn't talk, *really* talk, to anyone. Not since Danel."

"What was the order? The one she disobeyed?"

Liatra turned from him, groped without looking for a seat, her inner gaze fixed on something far, far beyond this moment. She sat silent for a moment.

"Termigan IV. The name means nothing to you, I'm sure. All right." Her voice grew crisper, outlining the facts. "There's another race in the galaxy. The V'ranyii. Twenty years ago, we discovered their existence when they attacked three League planets. When we forced them back, we found not one human alive on any of them." She paused, then added, "We didn't even find their bodies."

At the obvious implication, Rolen recoiled. Ignoring his reaction, Liatra continued. "Since then, we've been at war with the V'ranyii. We've pushed back their advance, and even found two of their home worlds. Termigan IV was one. It was Soleyla's first command, and she handled it brilliantly. Within twelve days, the V'ranyii had surrendered. They left their . . . hives, I suppose you'd call them, and put themselves in Soleyla's custody. All of them. Warriors, children . . ."

Her normally tranquil face clenched, and Rolen braced himself. In tones of ice, Liatra went on. "Then the order came from the Senate. Soleyla was to execute them. All of them. Even the ones who hadn't fought. Even the children."

Her shoulders shook, and Rolen clenched his fists against a sudden urge to reach out, to comfort her. "She didn't?"

Liatra shook her head, regaining control of herself. But her eyes, when she looked up at Rolen, were very, very bleak. "She pleaded. She stalled. She petitioned the Senate. Finally, she simply refused. Her . . . commander" — that odd pause again, Rolen noted—"didn't court-martial her. No. She was stripped of her pleasure slave, disciplined, and ordered to Antoros."

"And the captive V'ranyii?"

The answer was there in Liatra's eyes. Sickened, Rolen turned away.

And that's what they'd planned for Antoros, he thought bleakly. That's what they had planned for us.

His limbs were trembling with conflicting emotions. Horror, a sudden, dizzying relief, shame at the way he'd attacked Soleyla, cutting her to the quick at the very spot where, he admitted to himself, he'd *known* she'd be the most vulnerable. And why? Because she'd set aside what must be an almost unendurable desire to do exactly what he'd railed at her for *not* doing, instead clinging to a nearly impossible attempt to overthrow a hegemony which would order the wholesale slaughter of an entire people.

Termigan IV.

Antoros.

And he'd said she had no heart.

With a moan, Rolen sank to his knees, clasping his hands over the sounds that escaped his throat. His rage inverted, became a black self-contempt that filled him like venom, toxic and cold. It was only now, now when it was far too late to unsay or undo any of it, that he understood exactly who Soleyla had been fighting to preserve during the battle that had cost her Kantou.

Who could have guessed the world had so many pits to fall into? Looking back, Rolen saw his people as Soleyla must have seen them. Proud, innocent, painfully defenseless. Saw himself—headstrong, brash, and mortally ignorant. She'd sacrificed everything, *everything*, to protect them . . .

Liatra was moving her hands over him, her touch hesitant and unsure as she stroked his shaking shoulders, his bent neck, his bowed head. With a low, despairing cry, he dropped his cheek against her firm thigh, burrowing into the shelter her gentle touch offered.

They'd dragged him, fighting every step of the way, through the wide, echoing hallways of the Priory into a large, high-ceiling room that blazed with light.

Her office, Rachel Devarian called it. It was more like a throne room. Tall white pillars reached up to a lofty ceiling from which skylights let down beams of warm illumination. In winter, slaves kept the skylights clear, shuffling carefully along the icy steel girders of the roof as they shoveled the deep snows of the fierce Argulian blizzards away, so that the regent, far below, might be bathed in sunlight.

She had been sitting behind her desk, a massive thing carved of the rarest pemmin-wood that curved around her, cluttered with papers and viewscreens, connecting her to affairs on dozens of planets. The whole thing was raised on a dais, taking up almost a third of the room. The remainder of the room was carpeted, with couches and deep, comfortable chairs scattered about — an illusion of informality. Woe betide the senator or emissary who forgot herself and actually sank into one of those seductively soft chairs. Kantou remembered all too well the cold, bloodthirsty smile the First Senator would flash at such a mistake. It was the smile of a predator with its prey trapped, helpless, before it.

The couches, though, *were* often occupied — not, however, by visitors. As he'd been hauled in by two burly Guardians, Kantou had seen Davud bent over one of them, his small, firm ass tilted high in the air, giving the Regent an outstanding view as Hamas rode him steadily from behind. The Guardians averted their eyes — not, he was sure, out of any sense of delicacy — but Kantou caught Davud's swift, troubled gaze before the youngest of Rachel's pleasure slaves lowered his long lashes, hiding his thoughts.

And Rachel Devarian, looking up from her idle study of the two coupling men, had seen Kantou straining against the grip of her Guardians, and laughed.

He didn't know how long ago that had been, now. Hours, certainly. Maybe more. His throat ached with thirst, and his shoulders burned like fire. They'd stripped him and thrust him into the deep stone-walled chamber Kantou remembered so very, very well. Then they'd twisted his arms up and closed the shackles, which were attached by a chain to one of the low massive beams crisscrossing the ceiling, around his wrists. Then they'd left him there.

The blackness was so complete it felt almost like a mirage. His eyes kept straining into it, trying to pick out shapes, the outline of the padded spanking horse, the crisscross frame of the whipping rack. His eyes craved illumination so desperately they fabricated it—phantom flashes of white and a strange, sickly green blossomed in the darkness, illusory flares from his light-deprived retinas.

Kantou panted shallowly, trying to ignore the pain shooting through his body. He was tired, so tired, but if he fell asleep his legs would give way, wrenching his already overstretched shoulders, and the sudden knifing agony would bring him, screaming, back to consciousness. He'd already fainted once, and the twist of his tendons had brought him, shrieking, back to his feet, his legs shaking with weakness. He'd vomited, then desperately fought the heaving of his gorge. His throat was so swollen he could hardly breathe.

Hours ago. Maybe a day. Maybe two.

He closed his eyes. At least the darkness didn't feel so hideously empty that way.

He was no fool. He knew that this—the waiting, standing bound in black silence, the unending pressure in his arms turning by ruthless degrees into torture—was nothing. He didn't pray for it to be over, because when it was over . . .

Kantou swallowed in a throat so dry it felt like sand.

Strange noises echoed at times through the silence—distant clangs, the low groan of a compressor, the quiet scuttle of rats. The torment in his shoulders flared into agony, moved through that into a steady, white sheet of fire that sapped his will, eroded what little courage he'd managed to muster, devoured everything inside him until nothing existed, it seemed, but the pain.

He imagined he heard a movement, off to his right. Certainly there was nothing he could see in this blackness. Then it came again—a small, hesitant shuffle. Kantou shuddered. The rats. The rats were coming to get him, knowing it wasn't long now, just a matter of time. They'd wait . . . surely they'd wait till he was dead? He kicked out desperately, ignoring the renewed torture in his arms, felt his foot connect with something that gave a soft cry.

"Kantou?"

Kantou froze. A tiny flame blossomed in the darkness, seeming brighter than a supernova. He squinted, made out a wan, worried face hanging above the light. He croaked something—a question. The face floated nearer.

"It's me. Davud. Hold on."

The light seemed to drift to the spanking horse and settle atop its leather padding. Then something rattled above his head, and Kantou screamed as his arms fell, nerveless, to his sides.

Davud caught him as he crumpled, clapping a hand over his shrieks. "Shh! We're both dead if I'm caught here. Kantou . . ."

The young man's voice was thick with tears. Carefully supporting Kantou as best he could, Davud helped him to the bench. Kantou sank down gratefully. Davud's face was turned away from him, his slim, graceful neck bent in distress.

"Oh, Kantou, why did you come back?"

Kantou felt a desire to hug Davud reassuringly, but his arms hung like deadweight, unresponsive to his mind's commands.

Little more than a boy, Davud had been purchased shortly before Kantou himself. Kantou had occasionally wondered what had happened to the two slaves they'd replaced. There was an odd pecking order among the pleasure slaves, revolving around who got called most often to Rachel's service. Sheer brute strength was a part of it, certainly, but the slim, boyish Davud had quickly realized that Rachel's current infatuation with him could be used to hold the others at bay. Then, when she'd become fascinated in turn with her newest, long-haired slave, he'd retreated into utter submissiveness, doing whatever the others ordered him to. Until Kantou had stepped in — at least when Rachel wasn't around. At those times, they all obeyed.

Kantou had stood somehow outside this shifting play of power among the powerless, holding himself aloof. Rakkan and Los, the two most dominant slaves, had sneered and postured like gamecocks whenever he was around, but except when Rachel commanded them otherwise, they left him alone. And he had made sure they left Davud alone, as well.

Now Davud was here, risking his very life to free Kantou from his shackles. To no purpose at all. He could sneak from the cell, Kantou realized, possibly even get free of the Priory . . . but then where could he go? This was Argulus, the seat of the Nine-Star League. No planet was more closely guarded. He'd never get off it, and eventually he'd be caught and end up right back here. And Davud most likely would be killed.

He croaked again, trying to form words to tell Davud to lock him back in the shackles and leave. But the sounds that

14

came from his mouth were as cracked as his lips. "Hang on," Davud whispered, "I've got water."

Then something moist and cool and sweeter than any sugar was pressed against his mouth. Kantou gulped greedily, hissing when Davud withdrew the flask. "No, no more now, or you'll lose it all."

He was right, Kantou realized as the water reached his shrunken stomach. It twisted inside him, rebelling against the liquid. He swallowed convulsively, fighting to keep it down. The effort left him spent, trembling, too weak to talk.

Davud leaned against him, his soft brown hair brushing against Kantou's naked skin, and sighed. Kantou could feel his small, slim hands trailing over his chest, playing with the light sprinkling of hair there.

"I missed you, Kantou. Where . . . where did you go?"

Kantou shook his head dumbly, still unable to make his lacerated throat form words. They sat in silence, the two slaves, the younger one clasping the older one's hand like a child seeking reassurance. Slowly, Kantou's trembling eased.

"Do you feel better now, Kantou? You do, don't you?"

"Yes. Davud . . ."

"Good," Davud continued, and rose lightly, swiftly. "We've got to get you out of here." He tugged at Kantou's limp arm. When Kantou didn't rise, his tugs grew more frantic. Finally Kantou shook his head, and leaned back against the bench wearily. Behind him, the tiny candle flickered in a sudden waft of air.

"But . . . she'll *kill* you! I heard her talking. She laughed, you know, that way she does . . ."

His soft voice died away, conveying a horror deeper than any he could have spoken. *Yes*, thought Kantou. *That way she does . . .* She had laughed while Rakkan whipped him, laughed and then left him to Rakkan and Los to do whatever they liked with. And still he had not broken.

15

"Doesn't matter," Kantou slurred, his tongue feeling thick and unwieldy in his mouth. "Death . . ." *would be welcome*, he wanted to say. He couldn't get the words out. It wasn't death he was afraid of. It was what came before.

Davud knelt, gazing up at him earnestly, his delicate, almost elfin face contorted with worry. There was nothing Davud could do for him, Kantou knew. He jerked his head weakly. "Go on. Don't let her find you."

Shaking his head emphatically, Davud wrapped his arms around Kantou's knees, and laid his cheek against one long, lean thigh. "No. I won't. I won't. I'd rather die here, with you, than go back to . . . Oh, Kantou, can't we even *try* to escape?"

"Davud." Kantou fought his balky tongue, feeling the urgency of what he had to say. "Davud, listen to me. The woman who bought me — she'll be coming here. To free us. You. All of us."

Davud had raised his head again, his eyes wide with wonder. "That's impossible. The Guardians . . ."

"She *is* a Guardian. Davud, she'll do it. If there's a way, she'll do it." *If she's not dead*, he added silently, feeling his heart clenching against the idea. Soleyla couldn't be dead. She *couldn't*. "She's already freed Antoros."

From the blank look on Davud's face, Kantou knew the name was meaningless to him. "That's why," he continued, gasping to get the words out, "that's why you have to leave me. You have to live. So she can free you." He saw something flicker in Davud's eyes. It might have been hope. Or perhaps just disbelief. "Please, Davud. Go."

Unwillingly, Davud rose, nodding. "All right."

But as he turned away, the cell flooded with light, searing Kantou's eyes. He cried out, unable to raise his hands to his face to block the merciless brightness. Even with his eyes closed, it burned through his lids, sending explosions of fire into his brain.

16

Through this new agony, a voice spoke, cold and amused.

"So *that's* what my darling daughter is up to. Thank you so much for informing me, Kantou."

CHAPTER TWO

Liatra sat, almost paralyzed by the tremulous exultation inside her. Her hands shook as she reached, disbelieving, to stroke Rolen's raven-black hair. It slid through her fingers, thick, unruly, springing back up after her hand had passed. Like Rolen himself, she thought. It wouldn't be subdued.

You're the calm one, Liatra, her mother had always said—and for twenty-nine years it had been true. She was of a stolid, straightforward disposition, not given to tempestuous displays, soberly watching the passions of others with something between amusement and dismay. Let others have the dreams, the high-flown rhetoric—Liatra simply saw what needed doing and did it.

She was hardly calm now. Her breathing was labored, overloud in the still, silent room. A sensation like hunger, or a drowning man's need for air, was clawing at her breast, tightening her throat until she was almost gasping.

It was obvious that Soleyla had planned her capture of the advance base carefully. When she'd reappeared, dragging her 'captive' Antorean behind her, Liatra had seen the tension in Soleyla's stance, the wary, braced set of her shoulders, and known immediately the captain had something planned. She had dragged Rolen, trussed and half-naked, before the Guardians as bait—and they had taken it. Secure inside their plasteel walls, they'd descended on Rolen like predators, using him mercilessly, impaling themselves one after another on his unwilling flesh.

Liatra and Marda had assisted him as best they could as

the soldiers of the League's army had used his body for their own gratification. She'd watched him grit his jaw, his face rigid with determination, as he serviced them one after another, using hands and tongue and cock to bring them shuddering to orgasm, while straining desperately to hold back his own.

It was, of course, impossible. The third time he'd ejaculated Liatra had quickly moved to mount him, hiding the penis she was sure would remain flaccid, trying to stretch his life out a few more moments—for she knew, once he was of no more use to them, her fellow Guardians would dispose of him without a second thought. But as she'd ground her hips against his, simulating coitus, she was amazed to feel his cock stiffening again, nudging gently at the slick folds of her cunt.

Awed, Liatra had paused, staring down into eyes like the depths of midnight. A wild, dazed terror had lurked beneath their cobalt surface—a pleading that tore at her soul, shredding her defenses like tissue. In them she could see sensations flickering and cresting like waves. He was adrift in a vast, heaving void where arousal and exhaustion had fused into one, becoming a tsunami that had seized him in its unbreakable grip and would soon cast him, like a shattered toy, before the hungry swords of the Guardians.

Desperately, Liatra had held Rolen's gaze, trying to feed him strength, willing him to hang on, until yet another Guardian had straddled his face, breaking the contact. Thrusting her hips forward, the soldier had shoved her crotch against his tongue, her features thick with a greedy, contemptuous arousal.

Her expression had sickened Liatra. It was wrong. It was hideously wrong. She'd wanted nothing to do with this, this *abomination*, wanted to be a thousand light years away from it, wanted to drown the sense of uncleanness in the wide restless waters of her childhood, far away on Cetia VIII.

And she had wanted something else, too.

Liatra stroked Rolen's hair, murmuring softly. She was acutely aware of the void outside the ship, the endless, trackless reaches of space, filled with silence and great, burning masses of fire.

It was not, she thought suddenly, a placid universe. Even the cerulean waters of her home world which had seemed so constant, so unvarying in their restless, predictable motions, were aflame with life — microorganisms bursting into being, amoebae thrashing frantically through their watery world, fish and martok, crabs and jilbies all swimming and copulating, hunting and dying. Why should she be any different? Why should she, alone of all the creatures in the universe, think herself immune?

She swallowed, feeling saliva flood her mouth. For this was a thing she did not know how to face — that even in the midst of her disgust, revolted to her core at what was being done to the man beneath her, she had still felt arousal.

It was not, as it had clearly been for so many of her fellow Guardians, the rape itself that had excited her. No, the abhorrence she had felt was real and deep — but beneath it had been desire, hot and unmistakable. Desire and something deeper — and for that, she had no name.

It terrified her that it had no name.

What *were* these feelings? Never had Liatra felt so adrift in her own mind, as if her body, her very soul, had suddenly become a foreign land, a place she no longer recognized. She was lost within herself, within the emotions that rippled along her nerves and through her muscles, making her feel weak and yet preternaturally alert, as if she could sense the very molecules in her skin whirling in their infinitesimal dance, the cells in her blood rushing in an endless tidal roar repeating a single name over and over.

Rolen.

She would have sworn he hadn't the strength left to stand,

much less fight—and at first she'd been certain she was right, that he'd accomplish nothing more than getting himself killed. But the sheer courage of the gesture, as he'd hauled himself to his feet, had held her spellbound. Towering over her, naked, spattered with mud, he'd looked down at her, swaying on his feet—and Liatra had felt her tongue cleave to the roof of her mouth.

And then he'd killed Trika.

He was indomitable. Unsurpassable. And yet here he was, clinging to her, quivering, allowing her to touch him, to murmur soft, soothing, meaningless words, allowing himself to *need*.

A warm amazement bloomed in her heart, unfurling like some exotic flower, even as her blood beat with the sound of his name. He *needed* her.

Some voice of reason cautioned then, whispering in her mind. He needed, yes, but only for this moment, only because she was here and no one else was.

Do not want too much, Liatra.

She wouldn't, she thought fiercely, knowing even as she did that she was lying, that nothing, no words of reason or logic or warning, could ever stop the cry in her heart. If this moment was all she could have, then she would have it.

Gently, holding her breath, she cupped her hand across the back of Rolen's neck, and bent her head to kiss it. Her lips brushed lightly across his warm, tanned skin—and then froze as he stiffened, his muscles tensing under her hands.

"I'm sorry. I'm so sorry." Hurriedly, Liatra straightened, raising her hands to her flaming cheeks.

How could she have been so stupid? The man had been *raped*, brutally, forcibly, his own body's responses used against him. How, *how* could she have been so presumptuous?

Liatra dreaded what she would see in his eyes when he finally did raise his head—censure, reproach . . . judgment. She deserved it, however much she had loathed what was done to him. Had she stopped it? Had she even tried to stop it? She shifted restlessly, automatically trying to rise from her seat, to flee before she could see the condemnation in his gaze.

But instead, Rolen slid his arms around her waist, pinning her to the chair. Liatra watched in amazement as he groaned and dropped his head back to her lap, letting the tension run out of him like water. "No," he murmured. "No, stay." He turned his head, nestling his face between her thighs, and his next words were muffled, almost inaudible. "I need a woman."

Liatra tilted her head back, swallowing the flow of saliva that flooded her mouth, uncomfortably aware of the sudden, pulsing excitement inside her. As if summoned by his words alone, blood rushed to her groin, swelling the lips of her sex. He moved blindly, seeking, dropping hungry kisses up the length of her thighs. She could feel the heat of his breath even through the fabric of her uniform, could sense the trickle of moisture slicking her inner folds. Dropping her hands to his broad, powerful shoulders, she sighed, making no resistance as he spread her legs and nuzzled at the throbbing space between them.

This couldn't be happening. Not to her. But it was, and Liatra felt her heart winging from her chest like a captive bird turned loose. It didn't matter that he didn't love her. It didn't matter that she was convenient rather than chosen. She loved him, Rolen, the black-haired, indomitable Antorean who had risen from the mud to slay the one who'd tried to break him. At the memory of the sight of him, towering above her naked and unconquerable, Liatra moaned aloud.

Then he was lifting her, his hands cupping her ass, pulling her up with him as he rose. Awed once again at the sheer magnificent size of him, Liatra felt herself in comparison almost tiny, so effortlessly did he pluck her from the chair. She was hardly cognizant of him placing her on the conference table, his hands working insistently at her clothing until she felt her boots, then her pants, stripped away, and then . . .

Oh, and *then!*

Liatra had never so much as considered buying a pleasure slave. She could afford one, certainly, but it had hardly seemed worth the effort. Sex was just a need of the body, like air or food or sleep — you took it and went on to the next thing. Even when she'd availed herself of the rec slaves the League maintained for the use of its Guardians, she'd never been truly comfortable with the idea of telling a man how to service her — after all, she'd always thought it should be obvious what she was there for; should she have to tell them, too, every little move to make?

This was something so utterly different that she couldn't understand how it had the same name. She gasped as Rolen, kneeling on the floor, pulled her legs over his shoulders and dragged her to the edge of the table. Hungrily, he drove his tongue into her, his fingers, not stopping for niceties, spreading her engorged lips as he lapped and sucked, swallowing her juices. He devoured her, thrusting his tongue deep between her folds, his breath rasping harshly in his throat.

Liatra's head lolled loose on her neck, and she ran her hands through his hair. He shook his head restlessly under her seeking fingers, and she moved them, working his shirt off to stroke the rolling muscles of his enormous shoulders. She was strong, Liatra knew, her body robust and toned — but he was stronger. So very much stronger.

The knowledge excited her. *He* excited her, as no man had. He spread her legs wide and sucked her clit into his mouth with arrogant assurance, never glancing up to see if she enjoyed it, if she desired it. It was what *he* desired, and he took it. The tendons of her thighs ached as he shoved them further, but even that only increased her desire, pushed it up another notch. Suckling her clit with a fervor Liatra had never imagined, Rolen slid one hand down beneath it, flicked his fingers over her soft inner folds. The sudden jolt of sensation made her buck on the table, thrusting her hips upward. In response, he slid a finger inside her, then two, working them with some difficulty in and out of her opening.

"Gods," he breathed, his lips brushing her mons. "You're so tight, Liatra."

Then he *did* look up at her, and she almost came right then, simply from the sight of those midnight blue eyes. "You're not . . . I mean, you've done this before . . ."

Liatra surprised herself by laughing, a low, throaty sound that took them both by surprise. "This? No." She reached for him, drawing him to his feet. He didn't resist as she undid the clasp of his pants, sliding them down, revealing the erection that jutted, hard and thick, before him.

Liatra felt the laughter die in her throat, becoming something else entirely as she spoke. Her voice felt odd, almost as if someone else was speaking for her, someone who burned like the stars themselves, someone who didn't stand outside the lure of life's passions. "Nothing has ever been like this for me, Rolen."

His eyes changed then, the emotion in them becoming richer somehow, more complex. It was like looking into the depths of the galaxy itself, vast and immeasurable. With a hoarse, sobbing cry, he kicked his pants off the rest of the way and dragged her to him. Sliding one arm under her, he lifted her up, her thighs around his hips, her head cradled against his chest. One strong hand closed under her chin, tilting it back, and then his lips and tongue came down upon her mouth, claiming it as savagely, as greedily, as they'd claimed the opening between her thighs.

She raised her arms, sliding them around his neck, clinging to him like a vine to an oak — pliant, yielding, pressing her body against his. She could feel the hot throb of his erection against her belly, reminding her poignantly of the last time she'd been this close to him. Tears prickled in her eyes, and she squeezed them shut, praying that he wouldn't stop, wouldn't think of what had happened before.

Or perhaps that was exactly what he was thinking of. His lips tore against hers with an urgency, a desperation that left Liatra panting and breathless. One hand on the small of her back, one squeezing her buttocks, he raised her higher so that his cock pressed, hard and throbbing, against her slippery folds. Breaking their kiss, Liatra wrapped herself tighter, her chin resting on Rolen's broad warm shoulder. She whispered in his ear, feeling his unruly hair tickling her cheek, "Yes. Oh yes, Rolen, *please.*" And with one smooth, swift thrust, he plunged upward into her.

Liatra's head swam. She felt like she was being impaled on an iron shaft, held aloft by nothing but his cock and his hands. Blindly, mindlessly, she turned her head, nuzzling Rolen's neck, drawing lines of silken fire along his chin with her tongue. Her legs twined tight around him, she could feel the bunching contraction of his powerful hips, the tense and re-lease of his buttocks as he drove his cock in and out of her tight, waiting cunt.

She felt, more than heard, him groan, the sound vibrating through the thick column of his neck. He held her effortlessly, pinioning her against him, and she marveled again at the *strength* of this man, both physical and emotional. He was powerful, he was generous . . . he was far beyond her.

Only this, she reminded herself fiercely, *only let me have this!* This one shining hour when she could hold him, touch him, revel in the clean, masculine scent of him as he fucked her. It was enough, it was more than enough. It was ecstasy beyond anything Liatra had ever imagined.

"Please," she whispered again, barely hearing her own

words. "Please, Rolen, whatever you want."

At that he stilled, his cock slowing its smooth, intoxicating motions, and his hand on her back slid up into her hair, pulling her head back, forcing her to look up at him. Both abashed and excited, Liatra raised her gaze to his, unable to control the thing that shone in her eyes, the emotion she hadn't been able to name, to admit to—even to herself.

But her heart had flown away like a bird, and there was no denying anything anymore.

"Liatra . . ." He whispered her name, his lips in that small motion captivating her utterly. She watched them form words silently, an unspoken question she couldn't bear to answer. His body trembled beneath her clasped arms, and she cried out as he slid out of her and lowered her to the table.

His expression was troubled as he looked down at her. One huge, heavy hand stroked her thigh gently, over and over, as if trying to ease the sting of his words. "Liatra, I . . . So much has happened. I . . ."

She laid her fingers across his hand, stilling it, then drew it up to her mouth, kissing his palm. Slowly, trembling with need, she kissed the tip of each finger, nibbled lightly down their sides. She could hear his hoarse breathing, feel his hungry, anguished gaze on her, and looked up.

"I know," she replied. "Do you want me, Rolen? Right now, do you want me?"

His jaw was lax, his lips parted slightly. He was almost panting, she realized, his eyes dark with desire. Holding his gaze, she sat up, closed her hand around his still-erect cock, and watched his eyelids fall shut as he sighed at her touch.

Lubricated by her own juices, his cock slid smoothly against her palm, and she stroked the full length of it, enjoying its thickness, its hardness, the way the veins pulsed just beneath the sensitive skin. Rolen's head, she saw, had fallen back, exposing the column of his throat. She wanted to kiss it, lick the curve of his neck, his Adam's apple — but that would mean moving, and she didn't dare break the spell she'd managed to create.

Instead, she leaned forward, bending her neck so she could take Rolen's cock into her mouth. Saliva pooled under her tongue and trickled down his shaft as she closed her lips around the velvety head. Rolen groaned, and a sudden, blazing joy welled up in Liatra as she felt his hands move to her hair, stroking it over and over, like a man petting a cat, as she sucked him deeper into her mouth.

His gentleness was more than she could stand. After all he'd been through, after all the Guardians had made him suffer, still he could hold back, could let her take his cock at her own pace . . . It staggered her. And fired her determination, too. She *wanted* him to fuck her, wanted him to take the rage and hurt she'd seen in his eyes out on her body. But even when he'd been buried inside her he'd been able to stop, able to disengage, worried that he couldn't give her all that she wanted. Damn his scruples!

Liatra lashed her tongue against his shaft, over and over. Bringing her hands up, she caressed his huge, muscular thighs, cupped his ass, and pulled him deeper into her waiting mouth. Then, grasping his hips, she did it again, sliding him into her, *making* him fuck her. She felt his grip tighten in her hair, and whimpered longingly, letting her lips go soft and welcoming around his thick cock.

Slowly at first, then with increasing speed, he pushed himself into her. Liatra let her jaw loosen, giving him room to plunge all the way in and he took it, his fists closing in her hair, holding her still. Her body trembled, glorying in the sensation of being pinned in his grasp. Her groin ached with need, her clit so swollen it pulsed, longing for his rough touch, but she ignored it. It wasn't *her* gratification she was after right now. She wanted to drive Rolen so mad with desire that he couldn't stop, couldn't let go . . .

Lapping eagerly at his plunging cock, she sucked, feeling the surge along his shaft, the way his fingers tightened further in her hair. His thrusts became harder, deeper, almost choking her. *Yes*, she thought as she tasted the first salty tang of his juices. *Yes. Please, Rolen, take me!* Slipping one hand around, she slid it between the cheeks of his ass, tickling his rectum, and heard him growl as he slammed his cock home in response. Her other hand moved to his balls, cupping them lightly, feeling their round heavy weight brushing back and forth against her palm, enjoying the way the skin seemed to tighten over their hot, swollen curves.

His breathing was rougher now, labored. Smiling to herself, Liatra moved, letting herself slide from the edge of the table to the floor so that she knelt in front of him, her hands moving to his ass, keeping his cock in her mouth. For all his height, they fit perfectly — her head, when kneeling, was absolutely level with his crotch. Quickly, before he could think long enough to pull back, she thrust her head forward, ramming his shaft deep into her throat. Rolen growled, grabbing her head, and clamped his hands in her hair as he threw control to the winds and fucked her mouth. His strokes were deep, hard, almost brutal — everything Liatra wanted. No man had ever done this to her. No man had ever *fucked* her, forgetting everything but his own enjoyment. She reveled in it, in the way he pistoned his cock between her lips, in the first, hot spurts of come that flooded her mouth.

She sucked harder, urging him on, her fingernails raking his ass as he pounded her mouth, hammering his shaft into her. She felt him tense — her only warning — and then furiously, frantically, he ground her face against his taut belly, distending her jaw as he slammed his cock home. He held her tightly, forcing himself even deeper inside her as stream after stream of thick, burning come exploded from him, drenching her throat. She swallowed eagerly, hungrily, and felt him quiver at the pressure, his cock spurting again and again in a moment so perfect she wanted it never to end.

With a sobbing groan, he withdrew, and Liatra whimpered as his cock slid from her mouth. He fell heavily into the chair behind him and covered his face with his hands. His shoulders shook, and horrified, Liatra realized he was crying.

"Oh, don't, don't please . . ." Helplessly, she stroked at his calf, then moved so she was perhaps a foot from him, sitting on her heels as she leaned forward, longing to embrace him, terrified of how he'd react if she did. It would kill her if he pushed her away.

He shook his head, his voice muffled against his hands. "Liatra, I . . . How could I have . . . I didn't mean to . . ."

"To what?"

He didn't reply.

Hesitantly, ready to let go immediately if he stiffened or drew back, she closed her fingers around his wrists and tugged them downward, away from his face. He stared at her, his eyes like black hollows in his head, full of anguish and self- recrimination.

"Oh, Liatra, will you ever forgive me?"

Her brow wrinkled in puzzlement. "Forgive you what?"

"I . . . I *used* you. I treated you like a thing, like . . . like a pleasure slave . . ."

Ah. Suddenly, she saw. "Like the Guardians used you."

Wordlessly, he nodded, his gaze shifting away. More certainly now, she grasped his chin, noting the slight stubble that scraped against her fingers as she turned his face back to her. "Rolen, I wanted it. You didn't use me. Or, if you did, it was what I desired."

His eyes widened, a faint, grieving hope stirring within them. She nodded. "No man has ever made me feel what I wanted. No man has ever touched me like . . . like that. Please,

Rolen. Touch me again?"

He stood abruptly, turned away. Liatra stared at his back, feeling a sharp, knifing desolation stab through her. She'd disgusted him, so badly he wouldn't even look at her, revolted by her perversion, her submissiveness, her *need*.

But she couldn't help it. She couldn't stop this longing inside her. She wanted to belong to him, to be owned, possessed by this man who was everything — gentle and ferocious, unbreakable and tender. She would willingly lie at his feet, waiting on his pleasure, there for him whenever, *however* he wanted.

But he didn't. He didn't want her. She sobbed, trying to contain the sound, but it burst from her. At that he turned to face her again, looking down at her with compassion and something darker. His cock, she saw, was still half-hard, jutting before him. Everything inside her throbbed at the sight.

"I will not love you, Liatra, if love is what you want. Not now, not ever."

Silently, tears streaming down her cheeks, she shook her head. Love her? No. She would never expect that. It was enough if he would touch her, would allow her to serve him.

Still he hesitated, disbelieving, or perhaps just afraid. He was so tender of her feelings. She remembered how gentle his voice had been speaking to Soleyla, trying to reassure her. Oh, he was kind! Was he not worth everything she could give him?

And she would give him everything. Willingly, eagerly. If only he would take it. Holding his gaze, she bent slowly forward until her breasts touched the floor.

Then she dropped her head, resting it on the dense carpet, and tilted her hips into the air. "Please," she whispered. "Rolen, please fuck me."

CHAPTER THREE

Rolen stared down at the woman before him, her breasts pressed to the carpet as she thrust her ass in the air. Almost involuntarily, he circled her, studying her prone, motionless form from all sides. His cock had sprung back to attention already, twitching eagerly at the sight of her spread, gleaming ass.

Is this what Soleyla feels when Kantou kneels before her? This rush of sheer desire at the sight of him, awaiting her every whim?

Just as Liatra, he knew, was awaiting his.

No. It was wrong. No person, man or woman, should have such power over another. No one should have the right to use a human being however they saw fit. That was *slavery*, damn it!

Is it?

Rolen shook his head, confused by the conflicting ideas in his head. He remembered how he'd reacted when Kantou had faced him, declaring—*insisting* on—his right to serve Soleyla. His right to be submissive. Rolen had sneered, despising the man. And then found a carnal delight beyond anything he'd imagined in doing the same.

But *this*! Liatra was asking, begging, him to take her. To use her. To fuck her in any way, any position he desired. In—he gulped, feeling his shaft straining before him—any *place* he desired. He looked again at the soft, welcoming curves of her ass, raised, ready, waiting.

Rolen swallowed, hearing his pulse roar in his ears. A sense of power flowed through him, swelling his cock further, filling him with an almost unendurable lust. He wanted that, he admitted. He wanted to take her, devour her, fuck her in every imaginable hole, wanted to see her face suffuse with passion as he fulfilled every whim of his body upon her.

His jaw clenched. He would not do it. Would not become like the ones who had taken him, taking whatever they wanted, not caring what he felt or even if he survived. He would *not* be like them—no matter how much the idea might fire his blood.

But Liatra had looked at him with those steady hazel eyes and told him that was exactly what she desired.

Wracked by contradiction, Rolen stood, indecisive. Then Liatra whispered again, her voice reaching, coaxing. "Please, Rolen. Don't make me beg."

With a moan like the sound of a dam breaking open, Rolen sank to his knees, his cock brushing against her hot, moist sex as he did so. At the contact, an electric jolt shot through him, making his balls throb. He could come again, he thought wildly, right now.

Her hips nudged back against him, seeking, hungry. Grabbing one cheek of her ass, he squeezed it, heard her gasp in delight. Holding her firmly, he probed her tight, slippery opening with one finger. Her passage clamped down around him, tight as a virgin's, and Rolen felt his heart buck in his chest, sending a fresh wave of arousal through him. His cock was so hard he felt almost faint. Gods, it was almost more than he could stand.

And yet some eager, domineering part of him reveled in it. Some part he'd never admitted to, never realized existed inside him, rose up, demanding, making him growl between his teeth with a meaning utterly different than the same words had earlier, "Is this what you want?"

"Yes."

The word was a whisper. He smiled savagely, an

aggressive, feral hunger coiling in his gut. "Louder, Liatra. Tell me what you want."

"I want . . ." She hesitated, and Rolen pinched her ass. Hard. Then he took his cock in his hand, rubbed the tip of it back and forth across her dripping opening, teasing her, grinning when he heard her gasp. "Oh! I want you to fuck me."

"Is that all?"

"No. I want you to fuck me however you wish. I want you to fuck me, then make me lick your cock clean. I want you to split my ass open, if it's what you desire. I want . . ."

She stopped again, and Rolen, whose hand had frozen on his cock, afraid that if he brushed it against her one more time he'd shoot now, spilling his seed across her full luscious ass, drew in a ragged breath, then another, willing for control.

"What do you want, Liatra?" He asked it softly now, gently, holding his breath as he waited for her answer.

A moment ticked by, just long enough for him to note everything—the way his breath rasped in his throat, the pulsing ache in his balls, the heat emanating from her tight, willing pussy. And the way his entire body tensed, wanting to do everything she'd said, wanting to spread her, fuck her, possess her in every way a man could possess a woman. He wanted to dominate her, fill her, crush her in his powerful embrace. Wanted to feel her bend, yielding before him, taking everything he gave her, every pain, every pleasure, reaching her climax in the ecstasy of his commands.

Tense, expectant, he waited for her to speak. When she did, his eyelids closed, an emotion so hot, so overpowering flooding through him that he could barely remember to breathe.

"I want to be yours, Rolen. Your pleasure slave. Your toy. Amuse yourself with me, tease me, hurt me even. Command me to do anything. Anything you want."

He'd thought he couldn't get any hornier. He was wrong. Rolen dropped his hand from his cock, feeling his whole body rocking on the verge of orgasm. He wanted to savor it, linger in this all-encompassing sensation. He didn't dare move.

"Turn over."

Swiftly, she did, her gaze darting quickly to his face, widening at what she saw there, and then dropping demurely. She stretched on her back, her thighs spread before him, her cunt like a shining target between them. Rolen closed his eyes again, straining not to take her right then. Slowly, slowly, he let himself study her. "Put your hands over your head."

She raised her arms, thrusting her small, taut breasts into the air. Her eyes glowed with an ardor he couldn't deny. "Would you like it, Liatra, if I tied you like that? Bound you, helpless, before me?"

Her lips parted, her wet, agile tongue darting over them as she nodded. "Maybe I will one day. Now, touch your breasts."

As she obeyed, running her strong, deft fingers over the neat curve of her tits, Rolen could see a fresh wave of wetness trickle from her opening. "Squeeze them. Hard."

Her hands closed tightly around them, pushing them together, her thumbs flicking over their darkening nubs. Breathing rapidly, she writhed below him, lost in a rapture Rolen knew so well. But she would offer him more, he was determined, infinitely more than he'd ever given Soleyla.

"That's good, Liatra. Yes. Play with your nipples. Pinch them."

Her gaze burnt into his as she followed his directions, seizing the tight, tiny nubs in her fingers and twisting them. She gasped, and her hips rose involuntarily off the floor.

"Oh, you like that."

"Yes," she whispered. "Does it please you, my . . ." She bit her lip, suddenly uncertain.

"It pleases me. Now pinch them harder. Make it hurt, Liatra." Her mouth dropped open as she moaned at his words. Her fingers clamped down, and he could almost see the fire that ran through her, ignited by the sensation. He watched as she tugged them, squeezing, until she sobbed in combined pain and hunger. Her gaze fell on his cock, and Rolen became aware of his jutting erection, harder, fuller than it had ever been before. Gods! The things she was making him feel!

She was squirming before him, her hands working her breasts frantically, tormenting her nipples till they stood out like points, as erect as his cock. "Enough," he said lightly, and she froze, waiting.

"You would do anything I wanted you to." It wasn't a question. Her eyes answered anyway. "You would fuck anyone I commanded you to, just so I could watch."

Gulping, she nodded.

"Gods above, Liatra." He took a deep breath. "You make me wish I had shafts enough to fuck every hole you have all at once."

At that, a whimper escaped her, a tiny sound betraying an enormous need. He smiled gently, feeling a strange, possessive tenderness toward the steadfast, capable Guardian below him, a woman in whom loyalty, he sensed, ran very, very deep. Loyalty, and a wish to obey.

Grabbing her ass with both hands, Rolen flipped her over roughly. His cock poked demandingly at the crack of her ass, and he felt her tense, waiting.

No, he thought, smiling, *I'll save that a while.* Instead, he brought one hand down, hard, on her ass. She gasped and jerked below him, spearing herself on his cock.

She was so tight. Her inner muscles gripped him as hard as any fist, squeezing his cock. He shoved her forward, then dragged her thighs apart so she was pinioned below him, her ass spread wide, her body immobile. Inch by inch, he pressed himself deep into her fiery cleft. The pressure, squeezing him from all sides, made him clutch her hips, struggling to contain the orgasm pulsing in his balls. Her body shivered in pleasure. "Don't move," he snarled. Immediately she fell still.

Slowly, as the urgency backed off, he continued his leisurely exploration of her sex. Rocking gently, he teased her opening, pushing almost entirely in and then withdrawing, marveling again at the tightness of her as her passage crushed his shaft, making it ache. He was going to fuck her hard, Rolen decided, until the skin of his cock burnt with the friction, until she cried out below him and begged him for more. Rearing back, he tightened his powerful buttocks, and rammed his cock in one punishing motion in to the hilt. Liatra shrieked, and the sound impelled him onward, pulling out to thrust home harder, his hips grinding against her. His hands gripped her ass, pinching it, and he felt her push up against them, begging for more. Rubbing his thumb around the stretched edges of her opening, he gathered the moisture and spread it over her asshole, then pressed down, working the pad of his thumb inside.

Her pussy tightened in reaction, almost tipping him over the edge. Roughly, he pushed his thumb deeper, rotating it inside her, and heard her soft howl. "You want it harder?" he asked.

"Yes. Please, my master."

The word barely registered, so strong was his need. Dipping his thumb back to where his cock spread her open, he moistened it again, and worked it into her ass. Matching the strokes of his cock, he fucked her ass, feeling the pressure increase on his shaft. And even as he did, he was aware that this was what she wanted most, to please him, to be possessed by him, to be filled to overflowing until she cried out in climax.

His own craving heightened, and his hips pistoned faster, hammering his cock deep into her while his thumb drilled her ass. It must hurt, he knew, but her small cries made it amply clear that she wanted it. Straining above her, his balls heavy as lead with the come churning in them, he jabbed between her tender lips with a ferocity he didn't know he possessed. Beneath him, she arched her back further, wantonly shoving herself onto the hard, demanding forces invading her. "Say it. Say it, Liatra."

"Oh, Rolen," she cried, no hesitation now, "Oh, fuck me, my master, fuck me till it hurts. Fill my ass with your come, split me open. Fuck me hard, please, please, Rolen, please!"

Her body stiffened below him, her cunt spasming as she came, screaming. The sound of her begging filling his ears like madness, like honey. He fucked her ruthlessly, forgetting everything but the fire in his balls, the way her passage dragged at his hot, engorged shaft, everything but the white pulsing hunger inside him to devour her, fill her, drown her in his come.

His balls contracted with an agony sharper than pain, and he roared, smashing his cock into her, feeling his shaft buck and pulse as his semen poured forth in a furious, raging, endless stream that bore him along, drowning them both in ecstasy.

His thighs felt like water, trembling under his weight. Shuddering, spent, Rolen tumbled to the carpet, pulling Liatra with him. Her ass was still pressed against his spent erection, her head nestled on the thick swell of his biceps. He played idly with one honey-colored lock of her hair, tickling her earlobe, and felt her cheek curve as she smiled.

"Was that what you wanted?" His voice rumbled with amusement, knowing the answer, but wanting to hear her say it. Instead, she nodded.

"Tell me," he commanded. She giggled. The sound was doubly adorable from a woman who he knew was as deadly as he with a sword in her hands. Then her tone grew demure as she answered.

"Yes, Rolen. That was exactly what I wanted."

A warm, indulgent affection kindled in his chest, and Rolen pulled Liatra tighter against him, wondering if this was something close to what Soleyla felt for Kantou.

Immediately, his mood darkened. No. He knew better. What he felt wasn't even close to the fire of Soleyla's passions.

And he had shouted at her.

You never gave a damn about him, did you?

Remembering the way she'd left the room, upright, rigidly controlled, Rolen felt a pity so deeply it overwhelmed him. Where was Kantou, right now? Was he safe? Was he dead? He could forget those questions now and then, escape for a moment from their pounding urgency.

Soleyla couldn't.

"Tell me one more thing, Liatra," Rolen whispered, feeling her hair stir under his breath. She lay quietly in his arms, waiting. "Tell me there's at least a chance that we'll find him."

But this time, Liatra refused to answer.

Smiling at the sudden terror that froze him, Rachel Devarian stepped away from the wall. Slitting his eyes against the brightness, Kantou studied her—the same tall, upright carriage, the same thick hair like a blonde mane, the same patrician features.

But they were hardened in the mother to a chiseled, hawk-like cruelty that was utterly unlike Soleyla's clear, determined gaze.

How had he ever thought they were alike?

Davud whirled around, his face blanching, and the regent spoke, an indulgent lilt in her voice. "You did very well, Davud. Give him more water now. He must be able to use his voice."

His eyes cast to the floor, Davud knelt by Kantou, raising the flask again to his lips. Even as Kantou drank, he saw the flush in the younger man's cheeks, the shame that suffused his fine features and made his hands tremble, spilling the water.

Oh, Davud.

Rachel's smile deepened. Rakkan and Los stood behind her, grinning. With a gesture, she summoned Davud back, and he knelt at her feet, refusing to meet Kantou's gaze.

"You see, Kantou? Any slave can be broken."

Kantou could feel his eyes blazing with hatred. It would only make this worse for him, but he couldn't hide the rage burning within him. He had never felt any desire toward violence — even when he'd struck the Guardian outside the control booth, back on Antoros, it had never been his intention to kill her.

Now though, Kantou could have happily strangled Rachel Devarian, gripping his hands around her throat, tighter, tighter . . . He'd laugh, he thought, as he watched her face turn from red to purple to black.

If only he could raise his arms.

He spat instead, and spoke, enunciating clearly. "I'll tell you nothing." It was an empty defiance, and he knew it.

The First Senator laughed, a high, delighted peal that reminded him achingly of Soleyla. "Oh, but Kantou. You don't need to. If she's intent on attacking the League, it's only too clear where she needs to go. No," Rachel continued, moving closer until she stood over him, her face a mask of benevolent amusement. "I don't need your voice for you to *speak* with, Kantou."

Los laughed, a thick, cruel sound that stiffened Kantou's spine. Rachel glared at him, and he subsided immediately. Kantou could smell her scent as she bent over him, the breasts that were still high and proud even now, late in her fourth decade, on a level with his eyes.

"I merely want to make sure you can scream."

CHAPTER FOUR

Gripping her sword, Soleyla stood before the massive frame of Harth's main portal. Wide enough to accommodate the bulky refrigerated agri-drones used to transport large volume goods like grains and meat between planets, it towered over her, dwarfing the four other portals that ringed the shipping field. Before them, massed in eager battalions, stood all the slaves of Harth.

An urgency Soleyla could not entirely suppress flowed through her, tensing her muscles, sending adrenaline pumping to every cell of her body. On the other side of the portal, now growing increasingly opaque as it powered up, lay Marbul.

Harth had always been Soleyla's first objective. Close — at least in galactic terms — to Antoros, the agrarian planet was almost completely unfortified and largely uninhabited, except by slaves. One small Guardian base served as all the police force Harth ever needed.

Had ever needed. Soleyla smiled grimly. Surprise had been the only advantage she'd required to subdue the Guardians who'd grown soft and complacent in their less than onerous duties. And the slaves had flocked to her, as she had suspected they would. These were strong men, chosen for their size and the endurance to spend their lives toiling under the warm Harthan sun, planting, reaping, and sowing the crops that fed half a dozen more populous worlds. It was, in short, a recruiter's gold mine.

The slaves were her shock troops. She'd told them, bluntly,

that the death toll among them would be brutal. But each Guardian they felled would be one less for Soleyla's trained fighters who would land just as she led the first wave through the portals.

Marbul. It was the logical next step. The large, clement planet with its vast forests and low, rolling hills, was a major Guardian encampment, both training ground and barracks for the bulk of the League's army.

It was also the one place she might find Kantou.

Soleyla's heartbeat quickened with impatience. She suppressed it ruthlessly. She'd timed the assault on Marbul with a strategist's care. No word had escaped Harth of her attack — the first thing she'd done was knock out their comm tower — and so Marbul would be utterly unprepared for the ships descending in fire from the sky, just as the portals of its capital city poured forth wave after wave of newly-armed slaves.

If she took Marbul, she'd have crippled the retaliation that could not be long now in coming. Swift as she'd moved, by now a scout ship would be well on its way to Antoros to discover what had transpired. And as soon as it did . . .

So she had to act quickly, before the League could summon its forces. Liatra had signaled, twenty minutes before, from the skies above Marbul. Marda commanded the second ship, an aged freighter seized from Harth, both filled to the brim with stalwart Antoreans and battle-hardened Guardians.

They were ready. All the pieces were in place. The portal before her was brightening to a quicksilver shimmer.

And Kantou might still be alive. That was the thought which burned brightest in her mind, the desire that had driven her as she'd armed the slaves, biting back her impatience until she received Liatra's signal.

"Now!" Soleyla cried aloud and plunged through the portal. With a quick wrench of white, the world shattered. Then she was stumbling through the resistance that felt like heavy water, pushing through the barrier onto Marbul. Behind and around her, eager slaves crowded forward.

And died, shrieking horribly, on Guardian swords. Soleyla spun, fending off a vicious swipe. She glanced rapidly over the heads of her combatants. High domed towers rose in the distance—Marbul's capital city. They were there. They had made it. But what the hell?

At first she thought they'd stumbled by sheer bad luck into the midst of a training platoon, or perhaps a scheduled patrol. But as she looked at the melee swirling around her, the organized ranks of Guardians that converged on the slaves as fast as they cleared the portal, the sickening truth sank home.

They'd been waiting for her. She had led them, every one of them, into a trap.

How? How had the League *known?*

The question blazed in her mind even as Soleyla ducked under the murderous slash of a sword, came up to sink her own blade through her assailant's stomach, rip it out, and turn, her blade coming up again, to the next . . .

At her hip, the comm unit crackled. Liatra's voice was strained, desperate. " . . . der attack! Captain, we can't land! Repeat, Captain, we are under att . . ."

"Get out of there!" Soleyla roared—but she couldn't drop her hand to the unit, couldn't pause the half-instant a reply would require; she was fighting for her life against a press of deadly foes. Throwing herself to one side, Soleyla grimaced as the blade aimed at her sliced instead into one of the volunteers from Harth. They were dying like flies, untrained, poorly armed, against the best fighters in the galaxy. It was slaughter.

Too much, too soon. She'd tried for too much . . . and yet, what choice had she had? The emotion that filled her, as the sword came crashing down, was one of bitter, bitter disbelief.

How had they known?

Marda was ten times the navigator she was—Liatra would have been the first to admit it. And yet Marda's ship had fallen first, hounded into a boarding position by the relentless pursuit of the nine great ships that had risen like doom over the curve of Marbul's bulk.

Liatra struggled desperately, seeking an opening in the tightening ring. There was none. She cursed roundly, feeling Rolen's gaze on her. He was helpless now, out of his depth, unable to do anything but wait with the others as she battled the controls of the advance ship, trying to evade their attackers. The sleek ships had been hidden on the far side of the planet, behind the shielding mass of Marbul's two moons. With sinking despair, Liatra realized she recognized that trick—had been taught it, in fact, by the High Commander herself.

Amista had come, with all the wrath of the League behind her.

The two ships ahead of her converged, blocking her escape. Liatra veered to starboard, but the great flagship with the League's nine interlocking circles emblazoned on the hull was there, hemming her in. Like hunting dogs, the pursuers harried her into position, and Liatra wanted to cry with frustration as she released the controls. Other than a suicidal plunge into one of the combatant ships, there was nothing more she could do.

Ominous thumps echoed overhead, and tense faces stared upward as the grappling hooks clanged into place. Liatra felt frozen, unable to do anything but listen as the boarding tube was lowered, sealing into place with a metallic hiss.

This was the end. Of Soleyla's dreams, of her own newfound joy in a role the League would never allow her. Submissive to a man! She could imagine the contempt they would heap upon her, calling her a freak, a monstrosity, a pervert. Despising her for her aberrant desires.

Rolen was watching her, his eyes dark with apprehension. She could almost welcome death, at least on her own account—what shame was there in dying? But when she thought of Rolen, a rage deeper than she'd ever known seized her. Amista would not permit the same sort of 'sport' Valda had encouraged. No. The rebellious Guardians, and she herself, would be imprisoned, probably for life. But Rolen—and the other men—would simply be killed.

She would *not* sit waiting, frozen like a rabbit, to watch him taken away from her. She *wouldn't!*

"Come on!" Liatra bellowed and ran for the hull lock.

Rolen pounded after her. His men followed at his heels, swords drawn. The Guardians who'd joined Soleyla, whether out of faith in her, agreement with her cause, or merely from a desire not to be immured on Antoros, had followed more slowly. Liatra raced ahead of him, halfway to the lock. He could hear metallic thuds from behind it, as the League Guardians battered their way in.

Sprinting, he caught up to her. "Liatra, no! This is suicide!" Grabbing her arm, he spun her to face him, and was silenced by the feverish determination in her eyes.

It was there, it was all there for anyone with eyes to see. Her gaze was fierce, anguished—and the emotion beneath it was as clear as daylight in a desert. She was going to fight— not for the ship, not for her crew. For him.

And she was going to die.

Liatra broke his hold easily and dashed down the hall, drawing her sword as she ran. He saw the sparks as the door disintegrated, saw the swirl of Guardians pour out, saw Liatra disappear into their midst like a twig whirled away in a stream, her honey-blonde hair flying as she struck and struck and struck again, battling against hopeless odds.

For him.

Roaring, Rolen plunged after her, hearing his men close in behind. The two forces collided with a clash of metal, choking the hallway with twisting, writhing bodies. Ignoring a sword that slashed at his shoulder, he plunged through the knot of Guardians blocking his way. More crowded behind them, pouring from the boarding tube into the ship's corridor. He didn't stop to fight. Bellowing like a bull, he flung burly soldiers aside like chaff, searching the space beyond them.

"Liatra!"

She'd knelt in front of him, her forehead resting on the ground. Had presented herself to him, made her body into an offering that she'd laid, literally, at his feet. And he, furious at what had been done to him, nursing his rage and wounded pride, had told her he would never love her.

"Liatra!"

At the far end of the boarding tube, he saw a tall, upright, silver-haired figure. Commanding gray eyes caught his gaze, boring into him, and he stared, recognizing the distant figure as his true adversary. He battled toward her, Liatra's name like a battle cry on his lips.

It took nine Guardians to finally bring him down.

CHAPTER FIVE

High Commander Amista eyed the surly, massive man standing before her. Thick black hair hung over eyes that glared at her challengingly, despite the manacles on his wrists. It was, she noted, an unusual sensation, being regarded thus by a man. Had she been twenty years younger, she might have found it arousing, even piquant.

"Where is she?"

Amista stared. It was a look that had caused seasoned generals to flush. This man ignored it as if it were nothing—as if *he* were the victor here, demanding answers of a prisoner. "Where is she?" he repeated.

She gestured to a guard stationed near the door. Immediately, it slid open and Liatra, pale, a bandage over the gash along her arm, was led in. Something flickered in the man's eyes—relief, Amista suspected. Then it disappeared, hidden under a brooding impassiveness.

She turned to the woman. Liatra. Yes, she remembered Liatra Cor well. Had, in fact, observing the young lieutenant's stoic disposition and her tendency to attach herself to flamboyant, more assured leaders, trained her personally. A born second-in-command. Amista's lips quirked. Predictable that Liatra should have come under the spell of the tempestuous, idealistic Soleyla Devarian.

But it was the man she went toward now, her bound hands rising as if she would embrace him. With no more than a swift glance, he stopped her.

"And Soleyla?"

Again, he spoke, an occurrence so shocking it swung Amista's attention back to him. Amista looked again at Liatra, noting the way she stood back, as if it were this slave's *right* to speak first. Indeed, she was watching him with a questioning air, taking her lead from him!

There was much, Amista realized, she did not understand here. "Scala. Unbind them."

The Guardian captain, her personal second, stepped forward briskly. With two swift flicks of her wrists, she unlocked the rebels' restraints, and stepped back. Along the wall of the briefing room, soldiers tightened their grips on their swords.

"Please." Amista gestured to the table. "Something to drink?" Liatra nodded and sank to a chair. The man had not moved. "If I'd meant to kill you, I'd have done it already. Sit!"

His dark eyes flashed at the barked command, but he did so. "Why haven't you?"

Amista paused. In fact, she'd been ordered to. "I have my reasons." Demanding, that voice. Perhaps it'd have been wiser to speak to Liatra alone. But the high commander had been impressed by this giant of a man who, stripped of his sword, had still fought on, tossing the Guardians who'd boarded the ship like rag-dolls. And so she'd included him in this interrogation.

A mistake, possibly. Time would tell. She turned her attention to Liatra. "Lieutenant Cor, I am surprised, to say the least. I'd thought you'd have better judgment than this." Liatra paled, but remained silent. "To get embroiled in what is, essentially, a family quarrel—"

The man's eyes flicked to her face, surprised. Ah. He hadn't known that. What else, Amista wondered, hadn't he known?

"Soleyla was right," Liatra replied.

Amista raised one eyebrow.

Sitting forward, Liatra continued earnestly. "She was *right*, High Commander. What the Senate had ordered for

Termigan IV was—"

"Was *war*, Lieutenant." Amista's voice hardened. Wearily, she sank to a seat, feeling exhaustion like an ache in her bones. Into her seventh decade, now, she was. Fifty years of service to the League—outstanding service if she said so herself. Perhaps it was her own disquiet with the events on Termigan IV which had made her tone so sharp. She softened it now. "Soleyla had an order. She chose not to follow it and was consequently disciplined. That's hardly reason to start a revolution."

Liatra shook her head. "It wasn't just that. Oh, Commander, can't you see?"

"I'm trying to."

"What Soleyla did wasn't for Termigan, or Danel, or even Antoros." Amista's sharp gray eyes saw the man's shoulders stiffen at the mention of his planet. "It was because the League is *wrong*. Wrong in its very foundations. Our entire civilization rests on the subjugation of half its populace. How can that be right?" Liatra's hazel eyes were so very, very earnest. "And when Rolen—"

"Liatra!"

Liatra bit her lip at the man's barked word, and subsided immediately. Interesting. "That is you? Rolen?" The man returned Amista's gaze challengingly. "I'll take that as a yes. You don't act like a slave."

"I'm not."

"So I gathered. Antorean?"

He hesitated, then nodded curtly. "It's a beautiful planet," she said appreciatively. "I saw the holos from the first survey. I'd have fought for it, too."

The right thing to say, apparently. The tension in his broad shoulders relaxed, just a fraction.

"And so Soleyla went to Antoros, nursing a grievance against her mother's discipline. You didn't know?" Rolen shook his head. "Soleyla is the daughter of the First Senator of the League. A position it was fully expected she might aspire to herself, one day."

"*Is*? She's not dead, then."

Amista smiled. It was not meant to be reassuring. "Not yet. So you see, Rolen, you were merely a tool. A means to revenge herself against her mother."

Another flash of expression in those dark blue eyes. Doubt? Fury?

"That's not fair!" Liatra sprang to her feet. "Rolen, you *know* what freeing Antoros—"

"Liatra, be silent!" The Antorean had barked the words almost before she began speaking. Pale, near tears, Liatra subsided.

Very interesting. It seemed her instincts were right—as shocking, as unbelievable as it might be, this *man* was the power here, the driving force. Amista leaned back, studying him.

He returned her gaze with a level, steady stare, making his own assessment of her. Decidedly a unique sensation. There was no fear in him, at least not for himself. His tone had been peremptory, self-assured, *commanding* . . .

"Leave us." Amista glanced at Scala, indicated the guards behind her. "All of you."

"High Commander!"

Holding Rolen's gaze, Amista continued. "Take Lieutenant Cor with you." She'd watched him battling toward her, screaming Liatra's name. "He understands what the cost of harming me would be."

They left, Liatra gazing back at Rolen with a look of such naked hunger, such *need*, that Amista had to repress a shudder of distaste. She waited, unmoving, hiding her thoughts, until the room had cleared. "I need not remind you we're holding your men. Any violence against me would mean their

49

deaths."

He waved a hand brusquely, impatiently, as if to say he knew that already, get on with it. What he did not realize was that he'd just confirmed by implication what she'd already suspected — he was their leader. A man!

It took some getting used to.

Amista rose fluidly despite the fatigue in her bones. Circling the table, she poured a glass of wine, and held it out. Rising, Rolen took it. The high commander poured herself another, moved to a chair near the porthole.

Below, Marbul turned, the lower curve of its horizon spinning slowly into darkness. The prize Soleyla had sought — and if she'd seized it, her revolution might well have succeeded. Silently, Amista raised her glass, saluting the fiery young captain.

"I was, in fact, ordered to kill you, Rolen. May I call you that?" He stood behind her, silent. She could not see him, but she could tell he was listening.

"You, every slave, every rebel, every Guardian who'd joined her. And Soleyla herself."

"By the Senate?"

"No. By her mother." Amista glanced up, keeping her expression cool, neutral. "Surely you understand the military necessity of an undivided command. In the League, the First Senator holds that command."

"She ordered the death of her own daughter?"

Amista turned to him fully, let the revulsion she'd felt at that order shine in her eyes. "Yes. Now I want you to tell me why."

He did. He told her all of it, leaving out nothing. The way Soleyla had enlisted his aid, the seizing of the base on Antoros, the stratagem she'd used to achieve it. As he spoke of the rape, Amista's gray eyes had flickered, but he couldn't read their expression, couldn't judge her reaction.

She'd been ordered to kill them all, and she hadn't. And she'd put herself in a room, alone, with him. Unbound, unwatched. She was right, of course—he wouldn't have risked the lives of his men for a senseless, pointless revenge.

How had she been so certain he wouldn't?

He told her of Kantou, of the relationship between Soleyla and her pleasure slave. Even the sexual effect she'd had on him, Rolen. Even that.

Through it all, High Commander Amista sat listening, stopping him occasionally to question a detail, clarify a tactic. He told her about Valda, about the attack on Harth, the way the slaves, untrained as they were, had eagerly joined them, knowing it meant their death . . .

When he was finished, Amista sat silent for a long time, the wineglass forgotten in her hands. When she looked at him, Rolen saw an unexpected regret in her eyes. "You have no idea, Rolen," she said, her voice husky with emotion, "how much I wish I could have met you even twenty years earlier."

Rolen's first instinctive response was anger—was she trivializing him? Seeing him, even now, as no more than a sex toy? But when he looked again at the tall, silver-haired woman, her muscles still honed to the exigencies of battle, with lines of hard-earned experience surrounding eyes that had seen more than he had, so very much more, Rolen was surprised to find that same regret within himself, poignant and sharp.

What a woman she was. What a leader!

"You almost make me change my opinion of the League," he replied, his voice rough with a sudden, completely unexpected arousal, "if it produces such women as you."

Amista laughed delightedly. "A gallant barbarian! But no," she replied, the laughter dying from her eyes, "it is I, I think, who must change my opinions. About many things."

Hope blazed within him, wild and unanticipated. "You'll help us, then?"

Amista rose suddenly, went to the porthole and looked down. "No."

"But—"

"Rolen, I cannot." She turned back to face him, and in her gaze he saw the weighing of many things, of which Soleyla's revolution was only one. "I am High Commander of the army of a League which is still, despite all else, under attack from an enemy we do not understand. I dare not divert my forces to an internal dispute, which, simply by dividing us, could well be the death of us all. You must see that."

Rolen bent his head. He *did* see.

"Nor," she continued, her gaze roaming the room thoughtfully, "am I willing to see my command stripped away and placed on other, less capable shoulders. So, it seems the decision must be taken from my hands."

Rolen opened his mouth, but Amista held up a hand, stilling him, as she pressed a button on the comm, regarding him with a sly, almost playful smile as she spoke. "Scala, return to the briefing room, please." Again, Rolen found himself wondering what this woman must have been like at fifty, at forty . . .

Behind them, the door opened. Without turning, Amista spoke. "Scala, I am afraid we're being hijacked. The Antorean, as you can see, has taken me captive and seized control of the ship." Rolen's eyes widened. So did Amista's smile. "Despite my direct order to do so, you could not bring yourself to sacrifice your High Commander, and accordingly acceded to his demands. You will, of course, be disciplined severely later."

"Of course, Commander." Scala nodded alertly.

"Send Lieutenant Cor in. Oh, and one of those Antoreans to guard me."

Captain Scala withdrew, and Rolen waited tensely until Liatra appeared, looking confused — although not half as confused as Jerril, into whose hands Commander Amista thrust her sword. "You do know what this is for, don't you?" she asked. The poor fellow nodded. "Good. Don't use it."

Seized by some atavistic impulse, Rolen took her strong, wrinkled hand and raised it to his lips. In that brief contact he saw a flash, almost a vision, of an entirely different universe, one where he and she might have stood as equals, partners. Instead, he dropped her hand and they gazed at each other for a moment across a divide built of all the cold realities of their lives. Amista's eyes were suddenly very bleak.

"If you fail, young Rolen, I wish you a quick, easy death."

She watched him leave, Scala leading the way to the bridge, Liatra following behind. Sighing, Amista sank back to the chair, and waved at the nervous, blond-haired Antorean to refill her wineglass.

No, she thought, remembering Liatra's expression as Rolen had kissed her hand. She herself would never have followed him. Would never have worshipped the ground he walked on, the way the young lieutenant clearly did.

But she would have walked beside him. She would have been proud to do that.

Soleyla had asked for a few moments alone. Glancing at her grim expression, Rolen had nodded, and quietly withdrawn. Now she stood alone in the long dining hall, its empty tables and vacant benches seeming to call forth ghosts from the shadows.

She should be pleased, Soleyla told herself firmly. What High Commander Amista had done for them was almost beyond belief. Nothing now stood between her and her final objective. Nothing except shadows.

Why can't I cry?

The child-house of Marbul towered around her, echoingly empty. Marda, of all people, had volunteered to take the children born into slavery back to Antoros. They would have a life there—a chance at a life, at least. And Soleyla had more than enough navigators for the fleet now at her command.

The slaves of Marbul hadn't surprised her—not after Harth. They'd flocked to her by the hundreds, the thousands, massing before the nine waiting ships, shouting for a chance to fight for her. And she had the resources, now, to arm them. No, what had shocked her was the number of Guardians who'd stood among them, grim-faced and determined. Not half, no, not even a third of the massive army garrisoned on Marbul—but enough. More than enough.

She should be pleased, she told herself.

Here and there, she'd seen a Guardian holding hands with what was obviously *her* slave, shoulder to shoulder as they volunteered in her army, or bidding each other a yearning farewell. The sight had torn fresh lacerations in her already-bruised heart.

It was here, at Marbul, that Soleyla had always assumed the troops 'ported to Antoros had originated from—those same troops that had been slaughtered when Kantou had destroyed the advance base's main portal. The Guardian log-books had proved that assumption correct.

And it was here, if anywhere, that she'd hoped to find Kantou.

But there was nothing. No trace of him. If the smaller personnel portal had also been accessed from Marbul, no one had noted it. And no one had heard anything of a lost pleasure slave.

Why can't I cry?

At her command, wood from Marbul's vast forests had been piled in the center of the hall. Soleyla stared at it wordlessly, then thrust the torch she carried into its midst. Flames roared up, crackling in the dry timber. The air quickly grew overheated, sending beads of sweat rolling down the curve of her cheeks — the only moisture to touch them. As the flames reached the ceiling, Soleyla turned and walked out.

She had something to do yet, and so she must go on.

She strode from the building, climbed a nearby hill and watched as the building was consumed by fire. Sparks and ashes swirled into the night sky, taking the bitter remains of hope with them.

Finally she turned away. Behind her, the child-house blazed, a pyre to Kantou's memory. She strode past the others, barely seeing them. It was time to go. Time to finish this. She knew what had to be done.

The ship was waiting. There, she held conference in the briefing room, issuing last-minute commands to the Guardians staying behind to secure Marbul. Then, her back rigidly straight despite the exhaustion she felt, she went to her cabin and closed the door to find that one desolate, unanswerable question still awaiting her.

Why can't I cry?

CHAPTER SIX

On the screens ringing the pemmin-wood desk, images of violence unrolled like doom. Smoke, fire and bloodshed on half a dozen planets, and everywhere the advance of Soleyla's troops. There was rioting in the streets of Kasmalia, a shot of rebellious slaves tearing down a statue in front of the Priory on Cetia VIII. Even placid Bathun was awash in blood.

The port city of Argulus was under assault. Flames roared along the skyline as the largest contingent of Soleyla's forces attacked, slowly beating back the Argulian Guardians who fought them every inch of the way. It was only a matter of time, though, before the defense crumbled. And then . . .

Rachel Devarian smiled coldly. There'd been attempts at rebellion before in the long history of the League, just as tempestuous, just as heartfelt. All had failed, and the League still stood.

With its slaves.

She flicked off the viewscreens with one touch, raised her gaze instead to the far more pleasant sight of her pleasure slaves gathered before her, doing her bidding. Tren and Hamas had Davud on a table, the slim, boyish slave on his back, his hands tied securely to the sides of the table. Tren, his thick, solid erection jutting before him, straddled Davud's face as he held his calves, forcing Davud's slender thighs high up against his chest. Hamas, at the other end of the table, dug his fingers into Davud's hips, slamming his cock deep between the pinioned slave's ass cheeks. Davud strained his head upward, eagerly lapping Tren's huge, hairy balls.

A far, far more pleasant sight. Rachel Devarian smiled, clapped her hands once. Immediately, Hamas withdrew in one swift jerk, leaving Davud gasping, and came to kneel at Rachel's feet. She spread her thighs, gathered the white silk of her skirt aside and, grabbing a handful of Hamas's curly red hair, mashed the slave's face against her slit. He really had the most delectable tongue.

She gestured for Tren to take Hamas's place. The muscular, hirsute slave did so, gripping Davud's ankles and forcing them high in the air as he shoved his cock into the smaller slave's slick, oiled rectum. Davud's head snapped back as he shrieked in agony, but his erect shaft pulsed with each punishing thrust, bouncing against his flat stomach.

Perhaps today she'd allow him to come. Perhaps not. She enjoyed seeing his young face contorted with need as he squirmed, unable to touch himself. Once she'd caught him, his hands moving desperately over his cock, relieving himself without her permission. The red welts Rakkan had left on his smooth, white bottom had been really quite lovely.

Not half as lovely, though, as the second tableau she'd created, directly below her.

Rachel rose, pushing Hamas aside, and descended the two steps to where Rakkan and Los knelt, their hands tied behind their backs, facing each other. Between them, on all fours, unbound except by her will, a third slave rocked wantonly, alternately spearing himself on Los's long, splendid cock, and straining forward to suck Rakkan's shaft deep into his mouth.

The shining fall of his hair, though, was obscuring her view. Gathering it in her hands, Rachel played with it a moment, enjoying the heavy, silken feel of it sliding through her fingers. Perhaps she'd cut it off, just to see the look on her dear daughter's face.

Then she yanked it back, tilting Kantou's head up, even as his mouth worked greedily at Rakkan's cock. His eyes, those marvelous, complex gray eyes, gazed up at her drunkenly, glazed with arousal.

"Oh, you do like that, my pet." She ran her hands over his broad, scarred shoulders, savoring his fervent, heedless movements, and bent low to admire the sight of his lips, stretched to their limit around Rakkan's thick, rigid shaft.

"Harder, my pet. Show your mistress how much you want it."

With a deep, hungry groan, Kantou slammed his face forward, burying Rakkan's cock deep in his throat. She could see Rakkan tensing, moments away from flooding Kantou's mouth with jet after jet of thick, salty come.

Satisfied, the First Senator sank to a nearby chaise to watch at her leisure. Around her, the massive bastion of the Priory was silent, undisturbed by the approaching violence. Unconcerned, Rachel leaned back and gestured for Hamas again while behind her, Davud's shrieks became frantic.

Yes, she purred to herself with the predatory amusement of a cat. *Let her come. It's time my daughter learned a few brutal truths.* Rachel let out a low, anticipatory moan as Hamas's tongue stabbed deep into her sex.

Everyone could be broken. Even — *especially* — Soleyla Devarian.

Blood-smeared, sweaty, her face smudged with soot, Soleyla stood outside the Priory, watching as her forces herded the inhabitants out. Los, the last of her mother's pleasure slaves to exit, glared at her as he passed. Then, sword in hand, Rolen and Liatra flanking her, she ascended the steps.

Their footsteps echoed down the broad, empty hall. The Priory was silent, still, its gleaming white columns marching away in majestic indifference. At the far end, a clear light spilled out of the room beyond. Her mother's office. The tall doors stood open, revealing a glimpse of the raised dais, the enormous semicircular desk where the Regent of Argulus sat, intent on the viewscreen before her.

Soleyla's jaw clenched. So did the hand on the hilt of her sword.

For the moment, Rachel Devarian elected to ignore her daughter, her long, regal fingers tapping at a keyboard. Soleyla waited, unmoving. Beside her, she heard Rolen shift uncomfortably. She stilled him with a look.

"Well, Soleyla." Rachel hit one final key, and turned to face them. "Have you come home at last to visit your poor mother?"

She was dressed, Soleyla saw, in her favorite outfit — a soft white tunic over a white slitted skirt that gave glimpses of the smooth, taut thighs beneath. Her hair, as blonde as her daughter's, was piled high on her head, and her jade-green eyes glowed in a face that was still handsome and smooth. Soleyla could feel Rolen's gaze darting back and forth between the two of them, noting the uncanny likeness.

"No," she replied coldly. "I've come to arrest you."

Rachel laughed. "Oh, my dear, whatever for?" Her voice dropped, gaining an edge of menace. "It isn't I who've broken any laws of the League."

Soleyla gestured at the viewscreens. "The League is ended."

"Is it? And so you are the law now?" Rachel's eyes glittered as she glanced at the naked blade in Soleyla's hand. Returning her mother's gaze, Soleyla sheathed it.

"So righteous. My young, headstrong daughter." Nonchalantly, the First Senator leaned back in her chair, regarding them. "Tell me, Soleyla, did you ever stop to wonder why men were enslaved in the first place?"

Without waiting for a response, she swung the viewscreen in front of her around. Images played across its liquid surface as her mother spoke. "The planet we came from centuries ago. Earth. A beautiful planet, wasn't it?" Soleyla saw a fair blue orb, spinning within a soft cocoon of white clouds. Rachel punched a button, and the image changed. "This is what it became, under the rule of men."

Grainy, horrific footage rippled across the screen. Graceful cities toppled, their buildings sliding into rubble. Bodies lay stacked in ditches half a mile long. The blue seas turned murky, the sky darkened. A flash of light, so blinding Soleyla had to shut her eyes, ripped across the screen. In its passage, she saw an enormous city leveled—all in the space of a heartbeat.

"That's not possible."

"Oh, but it is. Have you never considered, for example, what a powerful weapon a spaceship's retrothruster could be? Can you imagine a tiny one, so small you could carry it in your hand—can you imagine what it would *do*?"

Soleyla paused. The military part of her could picture it, very clearly—and the implications.

"A formidable weapon," her mother continued, "until your opponent built a more powerful one. And what would you do then?"

Unwillingly, her eyes on the viewscreen, Soleyla replied. "I'd build a larger one."

"And so they did. Larger and larger and—"

"But why would they fight like that?"

Her mother shrugged. "Power. Greed. Ascendancy. Men have always fought for such things. It is their nature, coded deep in their genes. Castrating them helps but doesn't always solve the problem."

Thinking of the legions of emasculated slaves who'd nevertheless begged for a chance to fight, Soleyla paused. "Yes, but . . . If there's a reason . . ."

Rachel leaned forward, her eyes narrowing. "Tell me,

daughter, what reason justified *this*." She waved a hand at the viewscreen. "Mankind was on the verge of destroying itself when *womankind* rebelled. We overthrew the governments — all run by men — who would destroy their own species for their own gain. They cannot help it, Soleyla. It is in their nature, and we must guard them from it."

Rolen stepped forward then, his face dark with anger. "Then how do you explain Antoros? Shouldn't we be the same?"

Rachel Devarian looked down on him, sneering. "And have you never, Rolen of Antoros, used force to get what you want?"

"No!"

"Have you never in all your life fought with another man? Do your boys not bloody each other's noses for no reason at all? Have you never tried to take a woman against her will?"

As she shot the words at him, Rolen's face twisted. Soleyla could see him wanting to deny it, wanting to fling Rachel's accusations back in her face. And she could remember, too, the feel of him pinning her down, his hands tearing at her belt as he sought to . . .

"Enough!" she roared, stepping forward. "Even if it's true, how is it worse than condemning all to slavery for the actions of a few? You cannot convince me that every man supported *that*." She nodded brusquely at the viewscreen and folded her arms.

"No." Rachel shut it off and sat, looking pensive. "No, I suspect you're right, they probably didn't. But how else, Soleyla, could our foremothers have ended it?"

"I don't know. And it's not my problem. Now, will you come willingly?"

"To what? My execution?" Smoothly, unruffled, Rachel leaned back in her seat. "On what grounds am I to be tried? I am First Senator of the Nine-Star League and have carried out my duties in accordance with the law that bestowed them on me. Now tell me, then, daughter, what are my sins, exactly?"

Soleyla paused, then spoke, her voice hard with judgment. "You ordered the slaughter of the V'ranyii on Termigan IV."

"And what do you think the V'ranyii did to the humans on Rigel? On Carra? On Hort? The V'ranyii have retaken Rigel, by the way, while you were on Antoros."

"Another planet whose population you were willing to annihilate."

"Or assimilate." Rachel nodded equably.

"Enslave, in other words."

"The men, yes. That is our law."

"Then the law is wrong."

Rachel faced her calmly. "There are ways to change it, you know."

"How?" Soleyla cried. "Petition the Senate as I did during Termigan IV? File grievances, motions, while your Guardians massacre them? How many senators, Mother, would have voted against you?"

"Then elect new ones."

"In ten years!"

"Yes. Ten years is nothing in galactic terms, Soleyla." Rachel sighed. "But none of this is truly why you are angry with me, is it, daughter? You seemed to have no complaints about our form of government until I took Danel from you."

At the name, the confusion inside Soleyla coalesced into a cold, deadly rage. "You're right. I didn't." Tilting her head, Soleyla narrowed her eyes. "You never told me, Mother, what happened to him."

"Didn't I?" Rachel looked up, her eyes wide with feigned surprise. "Well, considering I am now, apparently, a prisoner of war, I can hardly see any advantage in giving such valuable information to my captors. If it *is* valuable information."

Furiously, Rolen took a step forward, gripping his sword,

but Soleyla held up her hand, stopping him short.

"Ah," breathed her mother, "perhaps we have something to talk about. But in private, Soleyla. It is, after all, a family matter."

Soleyla closed her eyes a moment, feeling the blood drain from her skin. Inside was a coldness so deep it felt like her bones were turning to ice. A sudden nausea gripped her, but she swallowed it. "No."

"No?" Rachel seemed amused rather than annoyed.

Soleyla folded her arms, her face set like stone. Inside her mind, a voice wailed. *Oh, Danel, forgive me!*

"No. You and I have nothing to talk about. Rolen, seize her."

But Rolen didn't move. Liatra was tugging at her arm, her words low and urgent. "Soleyla. What can it hurt? She can't escape. Where could she go?" She tugged again, and finally Soleyla looked at her, saw the concern in her clear hazel eyes.

Glancing back at the First Senator, Soleyla was certain it could hurt a lot—it was meant to. But Liatra was right. She *had* to know. She nodded once, sharply.

Rachel held up a hand. "I'll warn you, Soleyla, there will be nothing you can do about it."

Soleyla nodded again. If he is dead, at least I won't have to wonder. And if she kills me . . .

Turning to Liatra, she replied, "All right. Wait for me outside. If I'm not out in an hour . . ." She glanced at her mother and smiled wolfishly. "Use the ship's retrothrusters to level this heap."

It disturbed her deeply that her mother smiled back.

Soleyla waited as they left, then crossed her arms. "Well?"

Nonchalantly, Rachel Devarian rose from her seat, descended the steps to a low table, and poured herself a glass of wine. She gestured to Soleyla, offering, but Soleyla shook her head and watched stoically as her mother took her glass and walked toward the fireplace.

"I'd had such hopes for you, Soleyla," she said, running her hand pensively along the ornate mantel. "And to some extent, you've fulfilled them. You are strong, capable, not afraid to make the hard choices a leader must make. Who lives, who dies . . ."

"Get to the point, Mother." Her tone made the word an epithet.

"Patience, however, is not one of your virtues. You'll learn it, though, in time. As I did." Rachel sank to a divan, looked across the room at her daughter.

Soleyla watched her as one might a rabid dog. "Go on."

"Really, Soleyla, I don't know that I—"

"Go on."

"If you insist. Since you proved to be so fond of the V'ranyii, I 'ported Danel to Rigel."

Simply and terrifyingly, the world stopped in its tracks. Soleyla could see dust motes hanging in the air, unmoving, could see Rachel's eyes, glowing with a victorious spite. Then her mother's mouth was moving again, the words somehow slurred, slowed, sinking like liquid plasteel into her heart.

"They'd retaken it by then, of course. But the portal was still functioning." Rachel frowned. "I think."

"You bitch!" And then everything was moving far, far too fast. Soleyla's heart was hammering at her ribs as she lunged forward. A knife suddenly glittered in her mother's hand as Soleyla ripped her sword from her sheath. She tensed, expecting a throw, but instead the First Senator called out, "Pet!" and the door on the far side of the fireplace swung open. A man stood there, naked. A man with hair like a fall of silvery ash-brown silk, with eyes the color of an Argulian storm.

Soleyla froze, her sword poised in mid-air. Kantou. Her beautiful Kantou. He wasn't dead.

He wasn't dead!

A fierce, burning exultation rushed through her and every-thing else — Danel, her mother, her revolution — fell away. There was nothing in the world but Kantou's clear gray eyes, his beloved face. She started toward him, tears of relief cas-cading down her cheeks.

Why now, she wondered, *why can I cry now when I couldn't before?* In truth, the question didn't interest her. All she wanted was to touch him, feel him, impress the reality of him on all her senses . . .

Kantou glanced at her once, indifferently. His eyes slid past her as if she were nothing to him, a stranger. Then he walked to Rachel Devarian and knelt, tilting his head back at her touch on his chin, exposing his long, graceful neck. And Ra-chel, her eyes gleaming with enjoyment, laid the knife across it.

"Now, Soleyla," she said, looking up at her daughter, "I think we do have something to talk about, after all."

He *had* screamed, just as she'd wanted. Had screamed until his throat, lacerated with thirst, had shut of its own accord. But the screaming had gone on and on, inside, as she'd let her slaves use him, his arms tied high overhead, his pale, naked body completely vulnerable to their whims. They'd put clamps on his nipples, tightening them till he'd bled. They'd fucked him with their cocks, with dildos, with clubs. They came on his face, in his mouth, in his hair. And then they started again.

And all the while Davud had knelt at his feet, devouring his shaft with a desperate greed. His balls had grown heavy, aching, as Davud sucked him, until he didn't know where the pain ended, and the pleasure began. Each time he came close to the brink, Davud would pull back at *her* sharp command, and Rakkan would squeeze his testicles viciously till Kantou shrieked.

Once, he fainted, and swam back up to consciousness, wishing he hadn't, to find himself strapped over the spanking bench, his erection mashed agonizingly against the soft leather, while Tren slammed his fat cock deep into his ass. It burnt, and he wept. And still his cock pulsed, aching with urgency.

She'd laughed, then, delightedly, slid her hands up and down his shaft with a connoisseur's touch, driving him mad with need. Her green eyes had sparkled with lust, reminding him fiercely of someone, *someone* . . .

It began again.

She made him watch as her slaves serviced her, plunging deep into her spread, waiting pussy. He stood, his hands chained behind him, unable to touch himself or find any relief. Her cries filled his ears and his blood roared in his veins, making his massive shaft swell even further. Once, she'd sucked off Los before him, letting the big, muscular slave come in her mouth. Then, rising to her feet, she'd kissed him, letting him taste Los's juices on her agile tongue, letting him rub his burning erection against her, feeling the slickness of her wet folds.

Then she'd gotten on her knees before him, allowed him to press his cock against her hot, tight asshole. He'd strained in his bonds, desperate to pierce her. And she'd laughed, and laughed, and laughed . . .

Days. Weeks. Months, maybe—he no longer knew. He'd fall asleep in chains, dreaming of sex, to be awoken by a cock choking his throat, or barbed thongs whipping his ass, always rousing him to consciousness just before he could orgasm in his sleep. And so it began again, and again, never-ending, the pain and the lust blending one into another, and he couldn't escape it, he couldn't stop feeling, couldn't stop *needing* . . .

Until the moment came when she got out the whip and he

whimpered, not with dismay, but with arousal. He turned his ass to her, tilted it high, felt her run the haft of it down his spine, making him twitch with desire. She asked him questions, he answered, groveling, eager to please her, wanting whatever she wanted for him. No scream echoed through him, no memory of rage. Even his name had disappeared from his mind. He was simply *pet*, and he fawned like a dog, grateful whenever she deigned to touch him.

She'd placed the whip in his hand, nodded at Hamas. Willingly, expertly, he'd cracked it, reveling in the way her eyes brightened as she watched. And later she'd finally allowed him to come. As he'd rammed his enormous cock into Davud's tight little ass, Davud's screams had excited him further, making him drill harder, faster, enjoying their increasing shrillness. He'd peaked so hard his knees had trembled beneath him.

She was his lady. Now, and always. There was nothing before — there had never been anything before. She owned him completely, body and soul.

Whatever Rachel Devarian did, whatever she wanted, was right.

Soleyla stood, feeling her world crack around her. Kantou had looked at her, looked *through* her, as if she were nothing. As if Porto, and Antoros, and their night in the cavern hadn't even existed. His eyes, clear of shadows, had seemed shallow somehow, almost blind, robbed of the complex self-assurance which had withstood so much abuse.

Hoarsely, she whispered, "What have you done to him?" Her mother merely laughed, but Soleyla already knew.

Rachel Devarian had broken him. She had finally succeeded in snapping that formidable will. Soleyla noted the fading bruises, the signs of repeated beatings — but that wasn't what had reduced him to this. She shouted this time, the cords in her neck standing out, loud enough to shatter the very walls of her heart.

"What have you *done* to him?"

"Now, child, calm yourself," Rachel almost purred. "And put your sword down. It makes me nervous, and I'd hate for my hand to slip, wouldn't you?"

There was, of course, not the least trace of fear in her voice.

Shaking, knowing her face was ashen and unable to care, Soleyla sank to a couch, and laid her sword across her knees.

"That's better. Now . . ."

The knife was so bright against Kantou's throat. So bright, so cold, so sharp. He sat silent beneath it, patient, waiting. She remembered that silence, that patience. Once, it had all been for her. Only her.

"Anything," Soleyla whispered. "Anything you want."

Her mother glanced at her, her eyes harsh with displeasure. "Soleyla, I'm disappointed. You'd give everything at once, without even hearing my terms?"

"Name them, then."

"Ah, that's better." Rachel sat back, let the knife dangle idly as Kantou leaned his head against her knee. She patted him absently, stroking his hair.

Soleyla's palms ached with longing.

"First, you will assist me to restore order in the League." Soleyla stiffened. "Child, you may rearrange the universe however you see fit after I'm gone. I don't care. By then I expect you'll have learned better."

"No."

The knife came back up, pressing against the artery pulsing in Kantou's throat.

Soleyla closed her eyes.

When she opened them again, her mother was regarding her curiously. An emotion flickered in her eyes—it might have been pride. "All right, then. You win." Grudgingly, she added, "You do have some spine to you after all. Well, it appears that we have no more to say to each other." She lowered the knife to her lap. "Good day, Soleyla."

Standing unsteadily, feeling her body trembling with reaction, Soleyla asked disbelievingly, "You'll let him go? Just like that."

"Oh no, my daughter. Kantou stays. It's taken so long to get my pet trained just right. Hasn't it, pet?" She smiled indulgently down at Kantou and—to Soleyla's horror—he snuggled closer against Rachel's knee.

Stung beyond endurance, Soleyla brought up her sword. Immediately, the knife was back at Kantou's throat. The First Senator, Regent of Argulus, tilted her head, watching her narrowly. Furious, Soleyla spun on her heel. She'd come back. She'd storm this heap of rocks with a thousand Guardians . . .

"Soleyla!" Rachel's voice was sharp. "The second you walk out that door, your precious Kantou dies."

The threat in her mother's voice was real, and absolute. Soleyla froze in the doorway, her muscles quivering with rage. Frantically, she sought through her options—she could leave, and Rachel would slit Kantou's throat. There was no doubt in Soleyla's mind that her mother would do precisely as promised. And if she didn't leave—soon—Liatra would carry out her command. The Priory would be leveled. And Kantou would still die. Unless . . .

Unless she gave up her rebellion. Betrayed everyone who had fought for her, fought *with* her. She thought again of the Guardians she'd seen on Marbul, standing shoulder to shoulder with the slaves they loved as they'd signed on to her cause.

How well she understood the grim dedication with which they'd clung to each other, risking death for a chance at a life together. But for herself . . .

For her, dying was a certainty. But she would at least have the comfort of dying with Kantou.

Slowly, grimly, Soleyla turned back into the room, sank to a seat, and laid her sword across her muscular thighs.

Clapping sardonically, her mother smirked. "Oh bravo, my brave daughter. Dying for love of a slave. How heroic of you."

"Shut up." Soleyla rubbed at her temples, trying to ease the throbbing inside her skull. "If you kill him, Mother, you will die immediately."

"No. Really?" The sarcasm was obvious.

A minute ticked by. Another. Rachel Devarian smiled in triumph. "Would you like something while we . . . wait, my daughter? A glass of wine, perhaps?" Before Soleyla could answer she gestured, and Kantou rose silently. Pouring from the crystal decanter on the table, he carried the glass over and knelt down, his head bowed. Soleyla swallowed in a throat suddenly thick with longing.

Like this. Just like this, he'd knelt the very first time she'd seen him. In Merkun's tent on Porto, he'd knelt before her, his shining hair falling around his face like a veil, holding out wine.

"Kantou," Soleyla whispered. "Oh, my beloved." Reaching out, she touched him, felt his warm, scarred skin under her fingers. Unmoving he waited, seeming not to even notice her touch.

"Kantou. Kantou, *please* . . ."

He wouldn't even look at her.

"Enough!" Rachel clapped once and Kantou withdrew, returning to his place at her feet.

Bitter tears coursed down Soleyla's face. "You bitch. Oh, you bitch . . ."

Eyes glittering in triumph, Rachel leaned back on the divan and spread her legs. Horrified, Soleyla watched as Kantou, responding to the unspoken command, buried his head between her mother's thighs. His tongue lapped lazily, exploring her thoroughly, and Rachel's eyelids drooped in unfeigned enjoyment. "Yes," she hissed, "he is really quite talented. It's not hard to understand why you're so taken with him."

"But I'm being selfish," she continued, sitting up. Immediately, Kantou hunkered back on his heels, awaiting her pleasure. With a flick of her fingers, Rachel sent him to Soleyla. His eyes on the floor, he knelt before her, and Soleyla watched with growing dismay as his strong, clever hands worked at her belt.

"No," she whispered. "No! Kantou, stop it!"

But his fingers kept tugging, undoing her belt. Soleyla squirmed away, then stood. Like a spider, his hands kept crawling over her pants, unsnapping them, wriggling willfully down inside.

"No!" Soleyla roared, and backhanded him, hard. Kantou fell to the floor, and Soleyla gasped, her hands flying to her mouth, trying to contain her sobs.

Never, she'd promised. I will never beat you.

"Oh, my darling," she whispered, dropping to her knees. "Oh, Kantou, I'm so sorry. Forgive me, beloved. Please . . ."

Rachel laughed. The sound flayed Soleyla's heart even as she stroked Kantou's hair, willing him to look up at her once, just *once*. Suddenly she saw herself as her mother must see her — on her knees before a pleasure slave, begging . . . Soleyla flushed.

Bending low over Kantou, she reached back for her sword, held it before her as she wrapped one arm around him. "Big mistake, Mother." She smiled, and started to rise, pulling Kantou with her.

He wouldn't come. Mule-like, his head down, he stared at the floor and tensed his muscles. Soleyla struggled, straining. He was unmovable as a statue. Desperately, Soleyla brought

71

her sword up, slid it under his chin.

Eyebrows raised in surprise, Rachel Devarian watched silently.

Sobbing, Soleyla pressed the blade against his throat. If he wouldn't leave willingly, she would force him. It was better — surely it was better — than letting him die?

Her hand trembled. Every fiber of her being revolted against what she was doing. "Oh please, Kantou, *please . . .*" He *had* to move, *had* to come with her . . . Then he flinched, and a thin line of red trickled down his curved neck. Defeated, Soleyla slumped, dropping her sword with a clatter.

"Now," Rachel breathed, and Soleyla watched numbly, feeling her heart break anew as she realized Kantou's cock — his familiar, enormous, beautiful cock — was rigid with desire as he crawled to Rachel's feet. Reaching down, the First Senator caressed it lightly, and Kantou's head dropped back in an excess of lust.

Through her tears, she watched as Kantou serviced the First Senator, using tongue and fingers to bring her, panting, to climax. Anguished, horrified, she felt her body respond. Then Rachel slid to her knees and let Kantou fuck her mouth. Like a cat, she danced her tongue over the huge, meaty tip, and Soleyla could see the veins throbbing along his thick shaft. Her sharp, painted nails raked over his swollen balls, and Kantou groaned, thrusting deep into her throat, his hands digging into her mother's hair.

Writhing helplessly, Soleyla moaned, feeling the minutes pass, one by one. What could she do? She would not leave him, not even now. Wailing inside, Soleyla watched Kantou push Rachel back on the divan, following her signals, and wrench her legs wide as he knelt between them. His cock jutted before him, enormous, demanding. Rachel smiled again, her jade-green eyes gleaming. Turning her face toward Soleyla, she grabbed Kantou's hips, pulling them forward.

"Fuck me, my pet. Fuck me hard," she whispered, but her gaze remained fixed on her daughter's shattered expression. Her mouth opened in ecstasy as Kantou slammed his cock into her, pounding her mercilessly.

Something inside Soleyla cracked then. A blind, roaring darkness fell over her mind. Through it, she thought she heard the whine of the retrothrusters, far overhead. She no longer cared. Breathing was agony. Living was torture. The whine seemed to increase, or perhaps it was only her sobs.

With what she hoped would be her final breath, Soleyla threw her head back and screamed from the depths of her anguish.

"Kantou!"

He was adrift in shadows, empty, nameless. He had the sense that he'd been floating like this for a very long time—how long? He didn't know. He couldn't remember what had come before.

But there *had* been something before.

It was like swimming up through very deep water. There was a pressure inside him, like the body's imperative demand for oxygen. Only it was in his mind. The darkness around him seemed to thin and waver—shadows and light played before him, as if at the far end of a long, narrow tunnel. He pushed himself toward it, feeling resistance. But something nagged at him—something . . . If only he could remember!

Noises, now. Flat, muted. A sensation of heat in his groin. He was thrusting forward, again and again, pursuing a phantom memory through the lust in his body. Someone had called him, he thought. Who?

Pet. He looked at the word distantly with an unfeigned detachment. No. That wasn't it. He shook his head, sought on.

His balls ached with fire, a deep, straining need. Its pulsing immediacy echoed another sensation, another emotion, something hot, roaring . . . red. Red like flames, like blood . . .

Someone had called him. Someone had called his name.

Kantou!

The word burst into his mind, and with it, the roaring came into focus. It was coming, he realized, from his own throat. How he'd wanted to strangle her, hold her beneath him, watch her face turning purple! Rage pulsed in his brain, searing hot, and all he saw was red, and red, and red . . .

"Kantou, no! Stop it!"

Someone tugged at his shoulder. Shrieking in fury, he threw one arm backward, knocked them aside.

She lay below him, just as he'd imagined, hoarding the fantasy somewhere deep inside himself, twisted together with the memory of helpless frustration—*if only he could raise his arms!* And now his arms, obeying his command, thrust down. His hands clenched around her throat. His balls swelled as he squeezed, tighter, tighter still, his orgasm building like a tempest in his loins.

He was Kantou. Not *pet.* He was Kantou, *Kantou!*

Then hands, as strong as his own, closed on his neck, forcing his chin back until he looked up into emerald-green eyes.

"Kantou. That's enough." Soleyla held his gaze, her eyes intent and assured. "She can't hurt you any longer. Let it go."

Gasping, he released his grip, pulling himself out of Rachel Devarian's flesh with a shudder of disgust. Stumbling backward, he fell to his knees, quivering. Immediately Soleyla was beside him, drawing him close, tenderly stroking his hair. "It's all right now. It's all right. I'm here."

"Say my name," he begged hoarsely. "Please, say my name." She stroked his cheek, her eyes wide, drinking him in. "Kantou."

Over her shoulder, he saw Rachel Devarian shift, her hands rising to her bruised throat. Soleyla followed his glance, took his hand, then drew him up. "Come on. Let's go."

Pausing only to pick up her sword, Soleyla turned for the door. But as Kantou followed, Rachel shrieked behind them. Her ruined throat twisted the sound into grotesquerie. Seizing up her knife, she flew after them. Contemptuously, Soleyla knocked it from her hand, and it clattered to the floor.

For a moment, mother and daughter stared at each other. Then Soleyla turned away.

"Come on." Taking Kantou's hand again, Soleyla led him toward the exit. He strode forward eagerly, then staggered, dragging against her arm as he stumbled to one knee. Blood welled from a vicious slash across his back.

Soleyla spun to see Rachel, her mouth twisted in a vicious smile. The knife she'd retrieved glittered deadly fire as she drew back to stab Kantou again. Without thought or hesitation, Soleyla swung her sword in a flat, deadly arc. "Not this time," she hissed as her mother crumpled, lifeless, to the ground.

Chapter Seven

Frantically, half-dragging, half-carrying Kantou, Soleyla ran down the hall. The white columns seemed to stretch endlessly. Her heartbeat pounded in her ears, marking the seconds. Even as her fear choked her, Soleyla laughed in exultation.

They were free. Free! And if these were their last moments, they were still almost unendurably sweet. Even if they didn't make it . . .

But they did. Soleyla slammed through the doors, Kantou in her arms. Heedlessly, she threw herself down the Priory's broad steps, pulling Kantou with her, feeling sharp flares of agony as they tumbled against stone. She protected him as best she could, wrapping her arms about his head, but as they landed, the edge of a step caught his temple and he sprawled, pale and silent.

"Kantou! No!" Panicked, she felt for a pulse, but could hear nothing over the labored beats of her heart. Then someone was lifting her, bodily dragging her away from Kantou. She fought furiously as Rolen bore her away from the Priory, until she saw Liatra and Jerril running behind them, supporting Kantou's limp form between them.

High overhead, Soleyla heard a loud thrumming. "Come on!" Rolen yelled, and letting her loose, redoubled his pace. Then she was pounding across the broad concrete to where her forces waited, waving them frantically onward. Suddenly, she stumbled forward and fell, knocked flat by what felt like a wall of flame.

Superheated air whipped over her. She could judge what was happening by the looks on the soldiers' faces. Shock, horror and, distinctly, awe. Turning her head, Soleyla saw Kantou sprawled on the ground, shielded from the blast by Jerril's sturdy frame. Behind her the roaring grew, and Rolen met her gaze, his eyes dark with foreknowledge.

Soleyla nodded grimly, thinking of the awe in the soldiers' eyes. She understood, now, a bit of what Rachel Devarian had told her. The Guardians, watching the massive Priory crumble, would no longer be content with just swords.

Listening to the rumble of falling stone behind her, Soleyla imagined she heard the echo of her mother's cruel, mocking laugh.

It was hours before she could get away from the conference and return to the ship. At Amista's suggestion, Soleyla had included as many of the planetary regents as would come to Argulus, but by the ninth hour of listening to their fears, complaints, and various demands for primacy in the newly-formed League, she found herself wishing she'd exiled the lot of them to Kinrea. Only two of them were fit, in her opinion, to hold office, and those regents who hadn't come at all were stripped by proxy of their positions. The Senate would be composed, as it always had been, of elected representatives, but Soleyla summarily removed nearly all of the voting restrictions, demanding — and receiving — a League-wide one citizen, one vote system.

When they fell to squabbling over her requirement that one representative from each planet be male, Soleyla pushed back her chair in disgust. Twenty minutes later, she was at the ship, striding up the ramp to where Rolen waited, waving cheerfully.

"I came as fast as I could. He's awake?"

The massive Antorean nodded, then swung her into a bear-like embrace. "You've done it, Soleyla. You've really done it."

Scowling, she shook her head as she strode down the corridor. "They're still arguing."

"Doesn't matter," Rolen replied, grinning from ear to ear. "They came. Which means, Captain Devarian, that the revolution's over."

Ahead, Soleyla saw Liatra coming to meet them. Her eyes were turned toward Rolen, and it was to Rolen she went, wrapping her arms around his brawny frame. Soleyla glanced up at the black-haired Antorean and quirked an eyebrow. He grinned back at her, his expression embarrassed, almost abashed, before returning Liatra's embrace.

Jerking his head, he indicated a door down the hall. "Go on, Soleyla. He's waiting for you."

A strange diffidence overtook her, though, as she reached Kantou's door. She'd barely seen him since they'd fled the Priory, just a quick glimpse as he lay unconscious, swaddled in bandages, tended to by the League's best physicians. The sight of his ashen face had terrified her despite the doctors' reassurances. And she'd had no chance to return.

She should have been here, *here*, damn it! But in the chaos that followed the old League's destruction, every day, every hour, had meant bloodshed. Bloodshed that could be prevented. Urged on by High Commander Amista, she'd dispatched troops and messages all over the galaxy, hoping to stem the unnecessary turmoil and restore order quickly.

And left Kantou to awaken alone.

Now she found herself hesitating, feeling a curious reluctance to face him. She had promised never to hit him. Had sworn no one would ever harm him again. She had failed him in so many ways. Flushing with shame, she remembered the blood trickling down his neck, blood drawn by *her* sword.

What must he think of her?

Softly, she opened the door. His head was tilted back against the white pillow, his beautiful hair falling across it in shining waves. A thin cut, partly healed, marred the skin of his neck, and Soleyla stared at it, tears starting to fill her eyes. She had done that. No one else.

His eyes were closed, and his chest rose and fell smoothly. He was asleep, then. Soleyla was grateful for that fact. Quietly, she approached, drawn as if by a magnet. Every cell in her body seemed to yearn toward him, wanting to touch him, caress him, convey with hands and lips and limbs all the tangled emotions in her heart. Gently, her fingers trembling, she reached out, stroked a lock of his hair where it fell across the sheet, marveling at its softness, at the rich blend of colors it contained. Brown, yes, a smooth, shimmering chestnut, but there were streaks of gold amidst it, and a blond so fair it was almost silver. She'd never, in all their time together, noticed that before. How had she never noticed?

Wonderingly, she lifted the lock, running it between her rough fingertips. Like silk, like water, it ran through her fingers and fell back to the sheet.

She could not hold him. Not if he decided to go.

A tear ran down her cheek at that, followed quickly by another. Like twin raindrops they fell, splashing to the sheet, leaving two tiny round circles, four inches apart.

No, she would not hold him. He was free now, free to love, to leave, to live however he chose. That had been the whole point, hadn't it?

And she had done that. She, Soleyla Devarian. Nodding her head even as more tears spilled down her cheeks, she found that she could stand, could turn away, knowing that at least she had given him that.

"My lady."

His words were so soft she almost didn't hear them. She paused, her hand on the doorplate, and replied without turning. "No, Kantou." Then she *did* turn, bravely summoning a smile for him. "You're free now."

He didn't smile back. His eyes, dark and shadowed, regarded her earnestly. "And Antoros?"

"Will choose for itself whether to join the League. I suspect Rolen will encourage it to."

"And me?"

The question hung in the air between them like a lost bird, piping plaintively. Soleyla swallowed, forced a casual lightness into her voice. "And you . . . belong to yourself, Kantou. You are free." She smiled again, and turned away before her courage failed her and she broke down in tears.

As the door slid open, he cried out behind her, "What good is freedom then, if it costs me you?"

Soleyla spun back to see him struggling from the sheets, desperately trying to rise. The blood had drained from his face, and his eyes, dark with need, stared at her, beseeching. With a sob, Soleyla flung herself toward him, caught him as he crumpled, and lowered him gently to the bed. Her tears fell on him as he gazed up at her, raising a hand to touch her cheek. Then she was kissing him, blindly, desperately, covering his mouth and jaw and hair with kisses. Even as she clasped him to her, stroking his neck, his back, his arms, reveling in the touch of him, the sound of his glad cries as she caressed him, a terror, sharp and unfamiliar, clawed inside her.

For the first time in her life, Soleyla Devarian needed someone. Him. Kantou. "Don't leave me," she whispered fiercely. "Please, don't ever leave me."

Crying, she clung to him, feeling his arms wrap around her, cradling her against his chest.

"Never," he whispered. "Never, my lady."

She lay, listening to the strong beat of his heart under his warm, smooth skin. Raising her hand, she traced the cut on his neck with trembling fingers. "Kantou, I—"

He silenced her by taking her hand in his own, lifting it to his full, soft lips. Shivers went down her spine as he trailed his mouth over her fingers, bit lightly at their tips, turned her hand over to place a kiss in her palm. A deep, yearning ache rose through her in response, and she held her breath as he turned his head, gazing down at her.

The question in his eyes abashed her. She didn't know how to answer it. She ducked her head, focused on the motion of her hand as she stroked one lock of his hair where it fell across his broad chest, enjoying its silkiness, and the firm muscle underneath. Her fingertip brushed his nipple, and his chest rose as he inhaled sharply. She heard his heartbeat quicken and felt his cock stir under her thigh.

Panic shot through her, wholly unexpected. Her body felt awkward, clumsy, as she lifted her chin, bringing her lips to his. Their breath mingled as they lay, stiff and uncertain, their lips barely touching.

She didn't even know how to kiss him now. All the rules had changed. Hesitantly, she opened her mouth and closed her eyes as their tongues brushed against each other. At the contact, a wave of desire flowed through her, almost frightening in its intensity.

Kantou lifted her hand again, running his fingers over hers, weaving them together, studying her hand as if he'd never seen it before. "Soleyla," he whispered. "I . . . I don't know how to touch you. I want to. I just . . ."

With a rueful smile, she laid her fingers across his lips. She shook her head slightly. "Neither do I."

Lowering her head to his chest again, she ran her tongue over his nipple, feeling his hands come up to caress her hair. She sucked it lightly and felt a burst of triumph at his groan. Rolling onto her knees, she lapped her way slowly down the flat plane of his abs, then drew aside the sheet and licked his cockhead, marveling again at the sheer size of it. She caressed his thighs, running her fingers over the crisp hairs and firm, rounded muscles, then cupped his taut, swollen balls.

They seemed to pulse against her palm, hot and full, and she rubbed them gently as she nibbled at his shaft, working her tongue around the thick, meaty lip. She felt Kantou tugging at her pants, pulling them off. Then he drew her atop him so that she was straddling his chest, and clamped his mouth around her clit, suckling it, darting his tongue against the sensitive nub.

Pushing her hips back, she pressed against him harder, felt his tongue dive inside her, tickling her folds. Closing her hand around the base of his shaft, Soleyla raised his cock to her mouth, lapping the velvety purple curve of the tip.

God, it was huge. It pushed against her lips, so thick she had to open her jaw fully just to get the head in her mouth. Wishing she could take all of it, she sucked it, hard, felt as much as heard Kantou moan against her curls. The sensation was intoxicating, the sound vibrating along her clit, and she sucked harder. He responded feverishly, his tongue driving deep into her with a hunger, a *need*, that equaled her own.

His hands kneaded her ass, pulling her sex tighter against his face. As the heat inside her spiraled upward Soleyla straightened, drinking in the sight of his long, lean body stretched below her, his cock pulsing against his stomach, his mouth working hungrily between her thighs. Bending her neck, she stared down at his tongue flickering between the soft curls covering her mound, working her clit. Then he slid a finger inside her, and Soleyla rocked against it, driving it deeper.

It wasn't enough. She wanted him, all of him, wanted to feel his cock filling her, splitting her open. Sliding off him, she turned and straddled his waist, watching his face as she moved her hips downward until his cock nudged between her folds, prodding her opening.

He was looking up at her, his eyes wide and wondering. "Oh, Soleyla," he whispered. "Why is this so different?"

She shook her head. She didn't know. But it *was* different, more frightening, as if not only their bodies but their very souls were naked, trembling as they touched. His fingers shook as he opened her shirt, slid it from her shoulders, and caressed her breasts. "Please," he said. "Oh please, Soleyla, fuck me."

She watched him swallow as she pressed herself down onto him, feeling the head of his massive cock slowly invade her. It spread her wide, stretching her open as she pushed down against it, felt the lip spring past that resistance. Kantou's eyes were dark with lust, his eyelids half-closed as he panted, straining to hold back.

"Tell me again," she begged. His tongue flicked over his lips, and he squeezed her breasts, feeling the weight of them against his palms.

"Fuck me, Soleyla. Please. Let me inside you. Let me shove myself inside you. Please, my lady. Please." Tightening his ass, he thrust up beneath her, driving his cock into her. Soleyla's head rocked back, and she cried out at the mingled pain and ecstasy as his massive shaft split her open.

And still there was more. Rocking gently, he slid himself out, working just half of his cock in and out of her as she held herself still above him. His hands tightened on her breasts, and Soleyla leaned into his touch, staring down into his eyes as he played with her nipples, tugging them, then pinching their hard tips between his fingers. His mouth was open, his jaw slack with desire. "Yes," he hissed, "you like that, my lady."

Her head lolled on her neck as she moaned in response. His fingers tightened further, pinched harder, sending bolts of fire racing from her breasts straight to her core, igniting another spurt of wetness deep inside her. She could feel her juices trickling down over his shaft and her muscles relaxed, inviting him deeper.

His hands slid down her sides to rest on her hips. Watching her face, he pushed up gently. Soleyla closed her eyes, felt moisture flood her mouth. Gods, how she wanted him! He worked himself slowly into her, carefully, and she could tell he was holding back, fighting the urge to sink himself home.

But that was what she wanted, desperately. Her clit throbbed. She was right on the edge — but she wouldn't come. Not without him. Not until he threw aside control and fucked her with an abandon equal to her own.

Reaching down, she pinched his nipples, leaned forward till her breasts brushed his face. Groaning, Kantou opened his lips, drawing one nipple into his mouth. Rocking herself above him, Soleyla rode his shaft, dipping each time a little further, a little faster, until he moaned below her and grabbed her hips. Shoving her down against him, he thrust up, working his groin against her mound. Soleyla screamed and dug her fists in his hair, pulling his mouth more tightly against her breast.

He suckled her frantically, his tongue flicking her nipple as he drove his cock into her. It felt like she was being split in two, and *still* it wasn't enough. Sliding her hands under his ass, digging her fingernails into his cheeks, Soleyla rolled to one side, dragging Kantou with her till he was above her, her legs twined around his waist. Roaring, he threw his head back and drilled himself into her, pounding her as if he couldn't get enough. Wrapping her arms around his chest, Soleyla grabbed the mane of his hair, yanking it backward, urging him on.

"Yes, Kantou, yes. Fuck me, my beauty. Fuck me harder. Split me open." His shaft slammed into her, his balls mashed between the cheeks of her ass. Then Kantou shoved Soleyla's legs up against her chest and buried himself inside her. Her passage clamped around him, and Soleyla felt him stiffen as his cock swelled even further inside her. His balls, hot and hard against her ass, tightened, and Soleyla watched the lust in his eyes contract to agonized bliss, his face clenching as he came, flooding herewith wave after wave of thick, creamy fluid.

His cries filled her ears, tipping her over the edge and blindly, desperately, Soleyla reached up, pulling him down against her, feeling his pubic bone nudge her clit as he rocked, his cock filling every inch of her, pressing against the walls of her passage. Gathering her hair in his hands, Kantou pulled her lips to his, flicking his tongue between her teeth, and she moaned into his mouth as the world fell away beneath her and the hunger inside her exploded into liquid fire.

Gasping, they clung to each other. Soleyla could feel Kantou's heartbeat thundering in his chest, two inches from her own.

This is how it is then, she thought incoherently. *This is how it was meant to be.* She felt flayed, stripped to the bone, and yet fulfilled in a way she never had been before. Kantou panted in her arms, his skin slick with sweat, his breath tickling her neck. Slowly, he raised his head, the same sense of wonderment Soleyla felt mirrored in his gaze.

"Oh, my lady," he said. "Tell me I'm yours. Now, and forever."

Soleyla felt her lips curve in a smile. She drew Kantou down to her, and whispered in his ear, "Yes, Kantou. I am yours. Now, and forever."

EPILOGUE

A light, warm breeze tossed her hair as Soleyla stepped from the portal onto soft white sand. The feathery fronds of trees whose names she'd never learned rustled gently overhead. In the distance, the azure seas of Porto V glinted in the sunlight, and the riotous colors of the market tents gleamed before her.

Striding through the market, Soleyla breathed deeply, enjoying the tang in the moist, temperate air. Rolen strode beside her, his head swiveling as he stared at the pleasure slaves, posing wantonly before the tents, advertising their owners' wares. "Patience, Rolen," Soleyla murmured, her voice burbling with laughter. Behind them, Liatra and Kantou followed.

She led the way to a voluminous blue tent. The air inside was cooler, refreshing after the warm Portan sun. Two slave boys, too young to be sold off at market, greeted them courteously. One went to fetch Merkun as the other poured two glasses of wine and carried them carefully to Liatra and Soleyla.

Soleyla seated herself, and Kantou came to curl up at her feet. The slave stared, flabbergasted, as Liatra took the glass from his hands, handed it to Rolen, and proceeded to kneel by his left knee.

So did Merkun when he entered a moment later. The old man's eyebrows shot up almost to his hairline as he studied Liatra, her chin tilted demurely, her gaze dropped submissively to the ground.

"It's true, then." The ex-pleasure slave turned to Soleyla. "We'd heard rumors, of course, but the Regent of Porto barricaded the Priory, and hasn't shown her face outside it for days. Speaking of regents, do I address . . ."

His attention to etiquette hadn't changed in the least, despite everything else that had changed in the galaxy. Soleyla smiled and shook her head. "No. I am, however, First Senator of the newly restructured Nine-Star League. If you wish to greet the Regent of Argulus, though, you may do so."

Merkun's eyes glanced toward Rolen, then, disbelievingly, to the kneeling Liatra. Soleyla laughed delightedly. "Oh, Merkun, I thought you'd shed old habits easier than that."

Staring, Merkun gazed at the man sitting contentedly at her feet, his clear gray eyes glowing as he looked up at the trader.

Sinking to his knees, Merkun held out his arms to Kantou, tears running down his seamed, tired cheeks. "Oh, my child."

Kantou went to him then, and held the old man close. Merkun whispered, but Soleyla could nevertheless hear his impassioned words. "You were always my greatest hope, Kantou, my son."

Releasing him at last, Merkun looked up at Soleyla. "And what of Porto, then? What of the slave market?"

What of me? his expression added, but he was too proud to say it.

"Well," Soleyla drawled slowly, savoring the moment. A chuckle rumbled deep in Rolen's chest. "I'm afraid you're no longer a slave trader, Merkun. But your . . . protégés, I'm sure, will always find employment. After all, Porto is *the* planet for pleasure." She saw his eyes widen in comprehension. "You approve?"

"And they would be paid? Would be free to say no?"

"That," Soleyla said, rising, "will be up to you — Regent of Porto."

The old man, stunned, stared at her. Grinning, she strode

out of the tent. She could hear Kantou, as always, following one pace behind. Rolen and Liatra turned off westward, heading for a hostel, its terraces and decks festooned with vines and bright flowers. But Soleyla turned east and strode toward the beach.

The warm sands of Porto would be quite soft enough.

Reaching back, she grabbed Kantou's hand, dragged him up beside her, and twined her arm through his. He stared at her, surprised, and Soleyla leaned over, brushed his ear with her lips. "I've told you and told you, Kantou, I will have you. Where, when, and as I like."

Kantou's eyes grew smoky, darkening with arousal. She couldn't stand it any longer. She had to touch him, *now*. In the middle of the market, not caring who saw her, Soleyla pulled him to her and claimed his lips in a kiss.

"Yes, my lady," he whispered. "Oh, *yes*."

The End

DON'T MISS THE THRILLING PREQUEL TO THE DEVARIAN TRILOGY:

DEVARIAN PLEASURE SLAVE

Available June 2nd, 2023 at Extasy Books and many other booksellers.

Kasmalia is a far cry from the prestigious markets of Porto V, where only the most beautiful, most finely trained pleasure-slaves are offered for sale. On Porto, it is said, one can buy the best—but on Kasmalia, one can buy anything, no matter how depraved or illegal, an hour at a time.

The young, handsome Merkun, bound by his sex to a lifetime of slavery, nevertheless aspires to escape the clutches of the seamy brothel-owner who's purchased him. When she enters him in Kasmalia's annual pleasure slave contest, he manages to capture the attention of the Regent of Porto herself.

With his stunning looks, his unmatched sensuality, and sheer determination, Merkun quickly becomes her favored third in her ménages. But when he realizes he is falling in love with the woman who rescued him, can Merkun capture the Regent's heart, as well?

ABOUT THE AUTHOR

Dafoe has a thing for hot romantic heroes, cool ocean breezes, and — of all things — chickens. The day she figures out how to keep livestock on a sailboat, she's moving to the Caribbean.

An award-winning author who garnered three CAPA nominations in her first year of publishing, Sierra has gone on to receive numerous awards and recommended reads for her work. Her home on the web is sierradafoe.com, where you can find excerpts, sneak peeks, and all her latest news. Sign up for her newsletter for a special monthly contest!

www.ingramcontent.com/pod-product-compliance
Lightning Source LLC
Chambersburg PA
CBHW070522130626

46555CB00003B/1311